"What craft is that?" cried a voice from the deck of the ship.
"The Bow-wow-wow," responded Billy.—*Page* 96.

THE PIRATE'S TREASURE;

A Legend of Panama;

AND OTHER

AMUSING TALES FOR BOYS,

AND FOR

SOLDIERS AND SAILORS, ON LAND AND AT SEA

BY

WILLIAM H. G. KINGSTON,

AUTHOR OF "THE THREE MIDSHIPMEN;" "FOXHOLME HALL,
AND OTHER TALES;" ETC. ETC.

Fredonia Books
Amsterdam, The Netherlands

The Pirate's Treasure; A Legend of Panama; and
Other Amusing Tales for Boys, and for Soldiers
and Sailors, on Land and at Sea

by
William H. G. Kingston

ISBN: 1-58963-677-5

Copyright © 2002 by Fredonia Books

Fredonia Books
Amsterdam, The Netherlands
http://www.fredoniabooks.com

CONTENTS.

THE PIRATE'S TREASURE;

OR,

THE CAVERN OF PANAMA.

——•——

THE PIRATE AND HIS LADY-LOVE.

On the coast of that irregularly-shaped strip of land
which joins the two vast continents of the New World,
and is generally known as Central America, is a deep
bay called the Bay of Honduras. At the furthest end

B

of the bay is a narrow and long inlet, which, after a distance of some miles from the sea, again widens, and forms what is denominated the Gulf of Dolce; but it might much more justly be considered a lake, for such it appears in every respect to those navigating its waters.

It is a wild and sequestered spot, the scenery grand and majestic in the extreme. The western, or inner-most shores, are composed of almost precipitous cliffs, many hundred feet in height, beyond which appear ranges of blue mountains, of many fantastic shapes, amid which rises the burning mountain of Fuego, un-weariedly vomiting forth flames of fire and streams of burning lava, with showers of red-hot stones and dense masses of black smoke, which hang like a funeral pall over the scene of desolation and havoc. The sur-rounding country is, however, rich and fertile, and produces all the trees and fruits of the tropics. In the days of which we write it was inhabited by a powerful tribe of Indians, who had stoutly refused to bend their necks to the yoke of the bloodthirsty and gold-loving Spaniards.

In a sheltered cove, surrounded by thick groves of trees on the northern shore of the gulf, lay a power-fully armed vessel. She was anchored close in to the shore, and so completely screened by the foliage of the lofty trees, that she could not have been seen by any vessel passing outside the cove, had one by chance ventured thither, which was not probable, as the very existence of the gulf was unknown in general to Europeans, except to some of the roving bands of freebooters who at that time infested those seas in great numbers. The vessel was evidently being refitted, for her sails were unbent, her topmasts were struck, and her yards were on deck, while her crew were engaged, some on shore in front of tents making rope, mending sails, and shaping spars, and others on board in rattling down the shrouds, in painting her sides, scraping the masts, and other operations necessary to prepare her for sea. All her people were employed in one way or another, and all seemed working with a will as if eager to get what they were about finished with speed.

Near the summit of a cliff which rose at some little distance from the water, and overlooked the cove, sat a man, sheltered from the rays of the sun by a projecting rock. He was dressed in nautical costume, and more, perhaps, from the air with which he wore it than from the costliness of the materials, he was evidently of the rank of an officer. He was young, of a good figure, and had a handsome countenance, though it was much bronzed by the sun of the tropics, and furrowed by the storms to which it had been exposed—perhaps, also, by care and dissipation. "The *Serpent* will soon be ready for sea, and I shall find no further excuse for remaining here," he soliloquised. "My men are anxious to be once more following their wild calling on the ocean, and yet I cannot tear myself from her. I, whom once the very smell of the fresh sea breeze

would make frantic to tread the deck of my gallant
bark on the tossing wave, now sigh to remain on shore.
I thought not that woman had the power to enchain
me. Yet she is beautiful. A mind pure and fresh
from the great fountain source of nature, in a form of
angelic mould, so soft and feminine, yet so full of life
and animation, so joyous, and yet so earnest. That
beaming smile which plays over her countenance as she
sees me approach were enough to win an anchorite
from his devotions. How can I tear myself from her ;
and yet, how can I carry her away to live among the
rude lawless spirits with whom I am surrounded?
Then again, how can I be content to pass a life of
dull inactivity in exchange for the wild excitement
which has become necessary to my very existence? I
should sicken and die from idleness. I should do
wisely to see her no more, to hurry at once on board,
to get to sea at once,—the vessel might be ready by
the morning, — and endeavour to forget her in the
tumult of the raging battle. But then I should break
her heart ; I should be her murderer—I, who have
vowed to love and protect her—I, in whom she has
placed the full confidence of her guileless soul. But I
have also vowed to abide by my ship and men, through
good or ill, while our dark flag flies over the dancing
wave."

The speaker rose up, and as he stretched his arm
towards the spot where the vessel lay at anchor in the
bay below, he exclaimed—

"My brave comrades, I will not desert you. For your sakes I will quit all that has lately made life dear. For your sakes I will sacrifice——"

His words were cut short by a hand being laid on his arm, and by a voice exclaiming in his ear—

"What agitates you? Are you holding converse with the spirits of the air, that you thus speak when no one is by to listen?"

He started, his bosom heaved with emotion, and he threw his arm round a beautiful girl, who had stolen unperceived by him to his side. Her figure was small and graceful in the extreme; her costume showed that she belonged to the Indian race; her brow was bound by a circlet of gold, confining her hair, which fell in long tresses down her back; her robe was composed of feathers curiously interwoven, and a mantle of the same material was thrown over her shoulders, and fastened across her bosom by a clasp of gold, while her feet were protected by sandals richly ornamented.

"Tell me what you were saying, Hernan," she continued, in a soft musical voice, as she seated herself by his side on a rock from which he had risen. "You have been much agitated of late, and I must know the cause."

"Why did you come here to seek me, dear one? I told you I should return shortly," he answered evasively, for he could not bring his tongue to speak the truth.

"My father sent me to bring you to him. He is

anxious for your assistance at his councils," she replied. "But you have not told me the reason of your agitation, and the melancholy I have seen brooding on your countenance."

He gazed at her for some minutes without speaking, while her hand was clasped in his, and she looked up with inquiring wonder in his countenance.

He at length spoke

"Tara!" he said, "you see yon bark in the bay below, and those busy men. I am their chief, and bound to them by vows as strong as can bind man to man. I am what the world calls a pirate,—an outlaw; banished from my home and country; my hand is against every man, and every man's hand is against me. Poverty, with a proud and ambitious spirit, drove me to commit crimes, and hurled me from my position in society; wealth alone can restore me to that place. That wealth I can alone find on the ocean. Wealth gives power, and with that at my command I can return to my country, and set my enemies at defiance. Yon distant ocean is the field on which I reap my golden harvest. Some I have already collected, and a few months more of my hitherto successful career will enable me to amass sufficient to satisfy my utmost desires. Hear me, Tara. I will then return to you, and you shall accompany me to those distant lands as my bride. There, with your beauty and my wealth, wo will defy the envy of all who know us."

"What is wealth?" asked the young girl. "Have

you not here all you can desire? Is not my father a
chief? Has he not more power than any neighbouring
cacique? and does he not promise that when you are
his son-in-law you shall succeed him? Then why
quit me at all? I would go with you to the further-
most parts of the world; I would share with you
joyfully the dangers of the tempest and the strife, if it
were necessary; but surely that is not required. Oh!
Hernan, be content with what my father and I can
afford you, and seek not after what cannot make you
happier."

"Ah! little one, you know, happily, nothing of the
world to which I long to return. The power I seek
is over civilised men, with knowledge and strength
equal to my own. Gold is what I seek; jewels and
precious stones; those baubles which idiots value for
themselves, wise men for the power they give. If I
could find enough of such things to satisfy my wants, I
would no longer seek them on the ocean."

"Say you so?" exclaimed the young girl. "Then
promise me that you will perform all my wishes, and I
will place within your power such stores of gold, and
silver, and glittering stones, that you may become the
most powerful cacique of your country. There are
many dangers to be encountered before you can possess
this store; but your heart will not quail before them,
and I will share them with you."

"You are practising on my credulity, or are yourself
deceived," answered the pirate. "If this store you

speak of exists, others long ago would have possessed themselves of it."

"I do not deceive you or myself," replied the Indian girl, with earnestness; "indeed, indeed, I do not! The treasure exists, and shall be yours, provided you follow my directions. Promise me faithfully!"

"I promise to do as you may direct," said the pirate. "And now tell me how I am to find the treasure.'

"To-morrow, as the sun rises above the ocean, I will conduct you to where it lies concealed," answered Tara. "In the meantime, you must accompany me to my father, and say not to any one what I have told you."

Saying this, she took his hand and led him from the eminence on which they had been standing, by a pathway towards the interior of the country.

THE MAGIC CAVERN.

The ruddy glow which illumined the eastern sky, driving into the far west the shades of night, betokened the approach of the bright orb of day from out of the calm waters of the gulf, as two persons descended a narrow and steep path down the sides of the lofty cliffs which formed its western boundary. One was a man from the far-distant lands of the Old World, the other an Indian girl. She led the way down the dangerous track, and he followed in her unerring footsteps. The scenery was wild and rugged in the extreme. Above them rose rocks, black, and shining, and broken into a thousand fantastic shapes, reaching to so vast a height, that, as the eye gazed upward, they seemed to merge in the blue sky, while below them yawned precipices, over which an incautious step might have hurled them

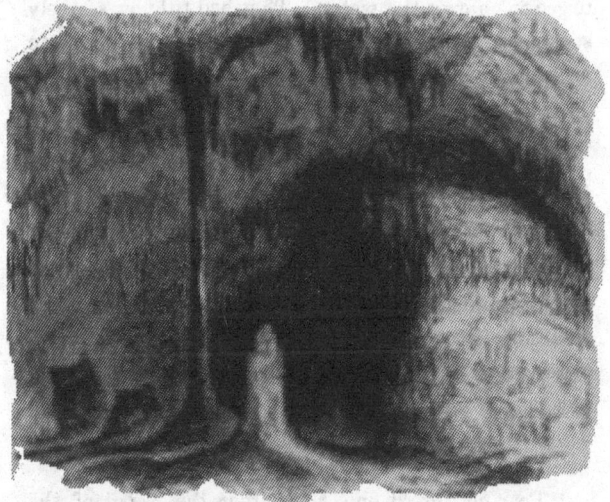

many hundred feet into the waters of the gulf below. Still they proceeded downward by many a devious turn, till at last they reached the very bottom of the cliff, where, to a ledge of rock forming the side of a small natural harbour, they found moored a light canoe.

The canoe was of a size capable of containing only

two persons, and such provision and tackle as the Indians generally take on their fishing excursions. The pirate chief unmoored the boat, and seating himself in the centre, the Indian maid took her place in the stern, when, with a light paddle which she held in her hand, she guided the course of the bark, while he urged it on over the water. They had till now scarcely spoken a word, for their whole attention had been necessarily engaged in descending the dangerous path.

"Our perils are now about to commence," said the Indian maid, as she impelled the canoe away from the rock. "What we have passed through is as nothing. If we enter the palace of the Spirit of the Tempest when he is aroused and angry our destruction is certain; but when the great god of our fathers, the bright luminary of day, rises, as he is about to do, in tranquil majesty through the clear sky, heralded by a calm lustre, as now, we have not much cause to fear: yet has he been known at times suddenly to become excited to fury and to destroy the daring intruders who have ventured into his realm."

"Fear not, loved one, that either the Spirit of the Tempest or any other spirit shall hurt thee. I am a son of the ocean, and have been accustomed to contend with them all my life. I defy them to harm us," answered the pirate, with a loud laugh, which sounded strange amid the solemn silence which reigned around, as it echoed from rock to rock, amongst which they were steering.

"I fear them not when you are with me," said the maiden. "But still I know their power, and the injury they may do us if we offend them. Therefore do not irritate them by speaking of them without reverence."

"Well, loved one, I will say nothing disrespectful," answered the pirate. "But tell me, how long shall we take to reach the Cavern of the Tempest?"

"Ere the upper edge of the mighty sun has risen above the water of the gulf we shall be at its entrance," replied Tara. "It is the proper time to venture within its precincts, for then the divinity we adore exerts his power over all evil spirits to protect his faithful votaries, and at that time his beams penetrate the inmost recesses of the cavern. We shall then also be better enabled to discover the entrance to an inner cavern, where the treasure we seek is stored."

The canoe had hitherto been passing along close under the cliffs, when Tara steered its course towards a promontory which projected forth some way into the sea, and hid whatever might be on the other side. The sun had not yet risen, but every instant the glow on the sky was growing warmer and warmer, and a glittering hue, the false edge of the great luminary, had already appeared, when, just as he himself arose, suddenly doubling the point, a scene such as it is impossible for words to describe broke on the sight of the adventurers. Above their heads, for upwards of three hundred feet, arose an arched cavern, like the portico of some mighty building, supported on either side by vast rocks, which seemed like pillars placed there by art, so admirably proportioned did they appear, while the whole roof was fretted by innumerable stalactites, which hung down pure and transparent as crystal, on which the bright rays of the sun now falling, made them seem of burnished and glittering gold. Arch beyond arch arose, ornamented with equal lustre, and pillar beyond pillar, while on either side were seen many fantastic shapes and forms, all shining brightly with the same golden hue.

There were temples with tapering spire and slender minaret; fortresses with tower and turrets, castellated walls and dungeon keep; palaces with innumerable windows and arched gateways,—every style of architecture was there. Nor were the forms of rural nature omitted. There were mountains and valleys, hills covered with villages, trees and waterfalls. Interspersed among them, too, might be seen gigantic figures of animals: the ponderous elephant, with his trunk and tusks, the slender-necked giraffe, the fierce lion and tiger, the horse and ox. Reptiles, too, were seen as if ready to crawl forth from their hiding-places; the crocodile and serpent, the toad and beetle; while birds innumerable seemed prepared for flight from the summit of some pinnacled rock; and the human form in every possible shape and character looked down from aloft. The monarch was there seated on his throne, with bearded face and sceptre in hand; the warrior with his bow ready drawn, or his battle-axe about to strike. Sometimes only vast heads could be distinguished, or human faces with bodies of animals. They were of all sizes, and many reached even to the lofty roof of the cavern; but the largest and most perfect of all was a figure of severe countenance, seated beneath a fretted and arched canopy, wearing a crown on his head, a beard reaching to his waist, and robes which seemed blown out by a powerful blast. In his right hand he held a staff, in the other a coil of rope. His head supported the roof of the vast cavern, his feet touched the water.

The pirate uttered an exclamation of surprise as he beheld this magnificent and beautiful scene.

"Behold!" whispered Tara, as she pointed to the last-mentioned figure; "yonder is the Spirit of the Tempest. He now sits enthroned in calm dignity, heedless of our intrusion. The staff he holds is to stir up the whirlwind and tempest; with the rope he curbs their fury when they have performed his bidding. We must offer a sacrifice at his shrine, ere we venture to proceed in search of the treasure; that must be sought for far up in the interior, beyond where the spirit sits enshrined, in deep gloom, in silence, and terrors unnumbered. See, that basket contains fit victims to sacrifice to the spirit of the tempest—fowls of the air, which wing their flight amid the raging storm towards the upper skies. We will hasten to reach his altar ere the hour of sacrifice has passed."

While she was speaking, the pirate had, at her bidding, again begun to urge on the canoe, which she

guided into the centre of the cavern. Not only were
the roof and every projecting part of the sides shining
with a golden hue, but the mirror-like surface of the
water reflected every pillar and pinnacle, turret and
tower, human form and shape of beast, with the most
perfect exactness, into the very furthest interior. It
seemed as if they were floating through a golden atmosphere within a globe of gold. Not a breath of air
was stirring, not a sound was heard but the splash of
the oar as it touched the water, and the ripple of the
canoe as it clave its way onward. Gentle as were
these sounds, they were echoed from every recess and
inlet of this wonderful cave, till they were lost far, far
away in the interior.

As they proceeded they could perceive long galleries
extending on either side, ornamented with stalactites
of so clear a nature that they reflected the light from
those which first received it from the sun itself, and
carried it far away from rock to rock till the same
golden hue was transmitted into the inmost recesses of
the cavern. No temple built by mortal hands, though
adorned with the most lavish expenditure that art
could suggest to captivate the senses, ever presented
an appearance to be compared with this in its su-
perb magnificence. The voyagers dared not to raise
their voices lest they should break the spell which it
seemed caused this magic spectacle; but Tara pointed
with her oar towards the god of storms, and thither
guided the canoe.

As they approached the foot of the mighty figure an altar was seen, with a flight of steps leading to it from the water, and at the back of it was a vast concave shield or slab of clear and polished stalactite. At last they reached the steps which led to the altar, when, fastening the boat to a projecting rock, they began their upward ascent, the pirate carrying the basket by the directions of the Indian maid.

Although at a distance the altar had appeared close down to the water, comparing it to the gigantic height of the surrounding objects, they now perceived that it was raised considerably above it. On arriving at the foot of the altar, the maiden took the basket from the pirate's hands, and putting it on the ground, drew forth two milk-white doves which she placed in freedom on the altar. At the same time her voice, with musical sweetness, first broke the dread silence which reigned throughout that subterranean region.

"Mighty Spirit," she said, "deign to receive the offering of thy humble votary, whose fathers for ages past, in the times of their power and glory, have worshipped thee faithfully, and protect her and this stranger from the perils which await them in the enterprise they have undertaken. Mighty Spirit, cheer our hearts by a sign that we may know whether thou wilt allow us to proceed, and wilt lighten our path amid the intricate turnings of thy temple."

As she uttered these words, the two doves, which at first had looked startled and confused around, spread

their wings and flew upwards, till they reached the
arm of the figure, where they perched securely, and at
the same moment the vast shield, which had hitherto
remained lustreless, brightened up with a glow of
fiery hue, like the sun himself, so that the eye was
dazzled at beholding it, and the glory it shed forth
added a still further lustre to the whole extent of the
cavern.

"Thanks, mighty Spirit, for thy gracious omen,"
exclaimed the maid, prostrating herself before the
altar, where she remained in silence for a short period.
while her companion, lost in amazement, could
scarcely collect his senses to comprehend what was
going forward.

On rising she took his hand.

"Now, Hernan," she said, "the treasure may be
thine, and we must hasten on to discover it ere the
bright light which is shed over the cavern has again
faded away."

Accordingly they descended to the canoe, and once
more embarking, continued as before their onward
course.

They passed galleries innumerable, ornamented by
the cunning hand of Nature with the same gigantic
and grotesque shapes as those first seen—all of the
purest stalactite; and some were so true to the form
of the living being, that it was scarcely possible to
believe that they had not life; indeed, as one after the
other they appeared from the recesses and galleries

where they were placed glowing with the glorious
brilliancy of the sunlight, they seemed as if they were
actually moving from their posts amid the waters.

As they rowed on, the thought of the vast treasure
which these wonders guarded recurred to the pirate,
and his eagerness to possess it increased.

"When shall we reach the cave where the treasure
itself lies stored?" he asked.   "I long to feast my
eyes on its glittering heaps, and to feel that at length
I possess that which will enable me to set my enemies
and all the world at defiance.   Tell me how we are
able to discover it."

"It lies in the hundredth gallery from the entrance
on the left hand," answered the Indian girl; "I have
been carefully counting them; we have already passed
sixty, and have forty more to reach before we arrive
at the spot."

On, on they went. The time seemed long to both,
for though they had ventured to speak, their hearts
were filled with an awe at the solemn grandeur of the
scene, which kept them generally silent. The pirate,
also, felt as if he was the subject of some magical enchantment, and could not tell whether any moment
the scene might not dissolve, and they might find
themselves amid a chaotic mass of ruin and darkness.
He fondly loved the Indian girl, and believed in her
love for him; and although he had unhappily very
little religious feeling, he yet was somewhat imbued
with the superstition general among seamen, espe-

C

cially in those days; and as he knew her to be a heathen, and had just seen her offer a sacrifice to a heathen divinity, he fancied that they might be especially subject to the evil influence of the powers of darkness. His heart, however, was not one to quail before any horrors which a man may face, nor was his arm unnerved by any fears of what he thought might occur. Gallery after gallery was passed, and at length they reached the hundredth from the entrance. There was little difference to mark it from the others, except that, whereas the sea ran through all the rest, this had a pavement of rugged rock considerably raised above the level of the water, with a flight of steps leading to it.

"In yonder gallery is the cavern which contains the treasure," said Tara; "but beware,—at its end is a frightful precipice of fathomless depth, towards which a smooth and slippery floor shelves gradually downward; and it is said that many who have attempted to possess the treasure have fallen down it. But let us hasten; while there is light there is no danger, and whatever your fate may be I will share it with you."

"Brave girl!" exclaimed the pirate, forgetting even his desire to possess the treasure in his admiration of her courage and devotion; "you deserve far more than I can ever give you; but we will onward."

They again landed; after securing the canoe and ascending the steps, Tara holding the pirate's hand, they proceeded, without let or hindrance, along the gallery, looking eagerly into every recess in expectation of finding the treasure. For some time this search was in vain, till, on turning an angle of the gallery, they suddenly came in front of a cavern with a larger entrance than the rest, and into which the blaze of sunlight being reflected, a heap of glittering treasure was exposed to their view, such as the pirate even in his wildest imagining had scarcely conceived. From the nature of the treasure it had evidently been placed there by human agency. There were chests filled to the brim with gold and silver coin, ingots of gold and bars of silver; there were heaps of plate, urns, and salvers, and every ornament used on the tables of the rich. Churches, too, had been robbed, and sacrilege committed; for there were crucifixes of silver, ornamented with precious stones, chalices, and other utensils used in administering the holy sacraments; there were caskets, also, of the most valuable jewels, diamonds and pearls, and sapphires and rubies, heaped together in wild profusion; indeed, palaces and churches, and rich argosies, had been ransacked to increase the store of wealth, which, after all the blood which must have been spilt to gain it, there lay utterly useless to man.

The pirate for some time stood silent with amazement, though his companion, valuing little what she saw, regarded it with comparative indifference.

"Here is an abundance of that for which you would peril life and happiness," she said; "more than enough to fill your ship and to satisfy the most greedy desires of your companions"

"It is the wealth of a kingdom," exclaimed the pirate. "Tara, we will bear it hence, and you shall be my queen. The *Serpent* will carry all that is here, or if not, we will send her back to bring it, for unless some one betrays the existence of the treasure, no person is likely to discover it. We will now carry to the canoe some of these caskets of precious jewels to secure some portion of it in case of accident. They are the most valuable, and might alone satisfy the ambition of many men."

"I will help you," said Tara; "but, ah! What is that? Fly—fly, while there is time! Come this way; not a moment is to be lost, or we perish!"

She grasped his arm, and as she led him towards the way they had come, she pointed to the lofty roof down which a dark shadow was seen gliding.

"See," she continued, "the Spirit of Darkness is taking possession of the domain, and if we hurry not from it while there is light we may be unable to find our way, and may be cast down some of the yawning precipices which surround us. Leave those baubles; what are they compared to life?"

The pirate comprehended at once the danger, and cursed his thoughtlessness in not bringing torches, but there was no help for it. He had, however, secured two caskets, and with those in his grasp he followed his guide. Slowly and surely the shadows descended from the roof, and what an instant before was bright and glittering now assumed a dark and horrid gloom, nor could any of the figures or columns be longer distinguished where it fell. With hurried steps they rushed towards the entrance of the gallery, for once in the canoe they thought that they should be comparatively secure, and the light still shone along the ground and some way up the sides. Yet every instant their danger increased. Downward the darkness descended, like some shapeless monster crawling from the roof, or as a thick mist covers the landscape; but this looked like something palpable and opaque, as if it would at last crush the adventurers with its weight. The Indian maiden trembled not, nor was dismayed. He on whom she had set her affections, for whom she had encountered the peril, was with her, and at the worst she could but die with him. Of his crimes she thought not; together they might wander over the pleasant hunting-grounds of the departed, and they should be happy. The pirate, who had faced the raging battle, the howling tempest, and death in a hundred different forms, was the one who felt most an undefined dread of the doom which he foresaw might be theirs. It was not so much fear for himself as grief for the fate of her whom he had induced to undertake the adventure; and he would a thousand times rather have been on the deck of his ship engaged in the hottest fight than where he then was. Such thoughts rushed through his mind as they advanced. Lower and lower descended the shade. At last the floor was alone illumined, when with a cry of joy from the lips of Tara, they beheld the steps leading to the canoe. As they had a considerable way to descend, they again emerged into the bright atmosphere. Tara quickly took her seat with the precious caskets, and the pirate seized the oars and pushed out into the centre of the main cavern. Their dangers were, however, far from over. An extraordinary change had taken place, and instead of being in a palace of brightness and glory they were now in a temple of gloom and horror; the very monsters and shapes which had before appeared harmless and grotesque, now assuming the most terrific and frightful forms, as if about to spring from their recesses and to destroy those who might venture near them. The pirate urged on the canoe with all his might through the water, steered by the unerring hand of the Indian girl; but even his heart almost failed him as he looked over the side, and thought he could see fierce monsters swimming round them in the dark waters which supported them. Murmuring sounds also assailed their ears with unearthly shrieks and wails, and the very atmosphere they breathed seemed foul and oppressive. Down, down came the mighty mass of darkness. In that also, as the pirate gazed upwards, he could perceive, floating slowly above them, hideous shapes, just distinguishable by their blacker hue. Every instant he expected to feel their cold slimy bodies gliding by him, and as the darkness reached him he bent down his head to escape even for another instant the coming horror. Down, down it came at last, sensibly and palpably: it reached their shoulders, it descended to the sides of the canoe, it covered the water, and the pirate felt that the most terrible of deaths awaited himself and his companion—to wander about while strength lasted in the intricate mazes of that vast cavern, and then to starve with wealth uncounted piled up near them. The occurrences of his past life rushed over his mind. " This is the punishment for my crimes," he muttered; but his proud heart refused to repent. Even thought, however, was quickly banished by what next occurred.

To add to the horror of the moment, there came forth from every gallery and recess a loud rushing noise with unearthly shrieks, and cries, and groans, and the hitherto calm water became violently agitated, breaking over the sides of the canoe, which, with frightful violence, was turned round and round as if about to be swallowed up in a whirlpool. Even the Indian girl showed her terror by the slight shriek which escaped her, and the daring pirate held his breath. The agitation of the water, and the whirling motion of the canoe, continued for some time, and then as suddenly as it had commenced the turmoil ceased; but what had once occurred might, they felt, happen again, and the Cimmerian darkness in which they were plunged was still more dreadful. At length the pirate relaxed the exertions he had made to prevent the canoe from upsetting, and gave way to despair. There sat those two human beings in a frail bark amid the black void, surrounded by unknown dangers. The pirate was aroused suddenly by the voice of the Indian girl.

" Row on, row on," she exclaimed, in a tone eager

yet suppressed with awe; "I see a glimmering star ahead of the canoe — it may serve to guide us to safety."

Her voice recalled the pirate to himself, and ashamed of his weakness, with renewed vigour he plied his oar, yet he was still as if struck with blindness, for his less clear vision could perceive nothing but darkness around. With intense eagerness he looked out to catch sight, if possible, of the light of which she spoke, for he thought that perhaps her senses might have deceived her. Indeed, he expected every instant to find the canoe striking against the sides of the cavern, or that they had gone up one of the many galleries he had before perceived; but still on, on they rowed without interruption. At last he became sensible, from the peculiar movement of the canoe, that she was carried on by a current, and by trying with his paddle, he felt further convinced of the fact. After straining his eyes, too, for some time longer, he perceived the star of which Tara spoke, close down, it seemed, to the water, and yet pale and faint. On still they went, but yet it did not appear to increase in size, or rather it increased so slowly, that nearly an hour elapsed before any difference was perceptible. It did, however, increase, and by the time another hour had passed away it had more than doubled in size and brightness. Weary as the adventurers became, they, after some time, began to recover more the usual tone of their feelings, and to exchange observations, but they were still incapable of anything like conversation. Thus the day, or rather what appeared to them the darkest night, wore on; hour, it seemed, after hour, passed away, and the light grew larger and larger, and brighter and brighter. What appeared to them most strange was, that they should not long before have reached the entrance.

"Surely by this time we should once more have emerged into the open light of day," said Tara; "we have already been a far longer time on our return than we were coming, and are still at a great distance."

"We were then in the bright light, and had hope before us," observed Hernan; "we are now in darkness, and shall feel grateful if we escape with our lives."

He spoke without remembering the caskets of jewels.

"But my weary arms and failing strength tell me that the day is wearing on and the evening approaching," replied Tara; "depend upon it night is not far distant."

"True, love, you must be right," said the pirate; "we have had a current with us, and the water when we came was apparently still. This cavern must communicate with some inland river or lake."

"I know of every lake and stream far and wide," replied Tara; "there are none near here which are likely to fall into the cavern."

"I cannot account for it, but that there is a current I am certain, for I heard it rippling against the sides

of the cavern," observed Hernan. "When we get
back into the gulf we shall be able to discover the
truth."

"Ah!" exclaimed Tara, "but perhaps the mighty
Spirit of the Tempest may have become angry at our
long delay, and may prohibit our departure. We have
many dangers yet to encounter."

"I fear them not, dearest, for myself, yet I grieve
to have brought you to encounter them," answered
Hernan; "but having escaped so many already we
may surmount the remainder."

While they were speaking, the star had been increasing more rapidly than before, and even a light
was perceptible throughout the cavern, though not
sufficiently strong to enable them to distinguish objects.
It was rather that the darkness was less black and
palpable than it had been. This change, slight as it
was, gave them renewed spirits and strength, and
Hernan plied his oar with greater vigour. The star
had now grown to the size of the moon, and went on
increasing; so did also the darkness decrease, and a
light, such as exists even in the most clouded nights,
appeared. This slowly grew stronger and stronger,
till the water on which the canoe floated was seen
moving, and a faint gleam of light played over it,
palely glittering on the bubbles caused by her rapid
progress through it, and the drops which fell from
the blade of the pirate's oar. Gradually the light
increased so much that the sides of the cavern came

forth to sight from the shade which enshrouded them; but how changed they appeared to the eyes of the adventurers! Instead of being covered with huge fantastic shapes, and perforated with long galleries, although here and there small glittering stalactites appeared, they were generally of smooth black rock, carved, apparently, by the hand of man, if it were possible to believe that man could have performed so gigantic a work. The width, also, was far narrower than before, though still probably the channel was some two hundred feet across. More and more the light came on, till the roof was also visible, when it was seen to be of the form of a regular arch, and to be composed of solid masonry of stones of vast size. Hernan had before been awe-struck with the magnificence of the entrance of the cavern as it had appeared at first; he was now surprised and bewildered, as much by the gigantic works with which he found himself surrounded, as by the wonderful changes which had taken place.

"This must be the work of enchantment," he muttered, "and witches have greater power than I thought, or else it is all a dream, the phantom of my senses. I cannot comprehend it."

The bright light of day now cheered their spirits, increasing as they advanced every instant, till, with a cry of joy, Tara exclaimed that she could perceive the entrance of the cavern, with the blue sea and sky beyond. Still the distance was very great, and to

their greater wonder they perceived a bright glow
descending over the semicircular space of sky before
them, till a blaze, like that of the sun himself, burst
on their dazzled sights, lighting up the mighty tunnel
far in the distance behind them. This circumstance
added still more to their perplexity, for that it was
really the sun they could not believe.

At length they emerged into a wild sea-worn cavern
of prodigious extent, the roof and sides composed, it
seemed, of black marble, rugged and broken in the
extreme. As they looked back they could perceive a
well-defined arch of masonry, forming the entrance to
the tunnel from whence they had emerged. It was
impossible to believe that the cavern was the same by
which they had entered, for whereas that was glittering with stalactites and full of light and brilliancy, this,
forming a perfect contrast, was on every side of the
blackest jet. The fresh air from the ocean came
gently into it, and the water rose and fell in glassy
undulations as it agitated from without and splashed
against the sides. Almost breathless with eagerness
and amazement, Hernan urged the light canoe swiftly
onward. The entrance to the cavern was passed, and
a new scene broke on their sight. The broad blue sea
was before them, glittering in the sunshine, the rich
sky glowing with a golden hue. On either hand,
headland and promontory appeared covered with the
graceful palm, the plantain, and the cocoa nut and other
trees of tropical growth, while among them in the

distance were smiling villages and detached cottages; and on the shores of the sandy bays were many fishing canoes, drawn up ready for launching. It was, in truth, a bright and beautiful spectacle, but unlike any view on the shores of the Gulf of Dolce.

"It must be; it is the Western Ocean, the mighty Pacific," exclaimed the pirate, "and we have come completely under the Isthmus of Panama."

"There can be no longer any doubt of it," replied Tara. "That cavern is called the Devil's Cave, and it is said that it is at night haunted by evil spirits; and now, as I gaze on those shores, I recognise many spots I know well. Look there, too, the sun himself is sinking into the ocean, a stronger proof that we are looking towards the west."

"It is, indeed, very wonderful; and for your sake, my Tara, I rejoice that we have escaped so many dangers," said Hernan. "We must now devise the best means of returning, for my men will be impatient if they do not hear of me."

"We will row towards yon village to the north," replied the Indian girl; "the people are faithful subjects of my father, and will gladly receive us. To-morrow we will commence our journey towards the east. We will not, however, venture again through the cavern."

The pirate agreed to her proposal, and towards the shore, therefore, they steered their course. They were received there with the warmest expressions of affection by the people, who were devotedly attached to their Cacique Omru, the father of Tara.

The following morning, accompanied by half the population of the village, they were on their way to the capital of Omru, which lay directly in their route. They had wisely forborne to mention their adventures to the people, and thus it was generally believed that they had come overland by a different route; nor was any one made acquainted with the existence of the cavern of Panama and its many wonders.

THE SAGE'S TALE.

Tara sat at the feet of her father, the Cacique Omru, and recounted her adventures in the magic cavern. On one side of him stood the pirate Hernan,—on the other, an aged man with a grave countenance and a white beard.

"Now listen," said the old man. "In the early ages of the world this country was inhabited by men of

mighty stature, who came in a floating house from the
distant regions of the setting sun. They were six
times as high as any men of the present day, and ten
times as strong, and twelve times as wise in worldly
wisdom; but they prided themselves on their stature,
and their strength, and their wisdom, and despised the
immortal powers which made them, so they dwindled
away in size, their strength departed, and their wisdom
became folly, and they perished from the face of the
earth. Ere they yet had become foolish they built
mighty cities, vast palaces, and gorgeous temples; but
the temples were dedicated to the Spirits of Darkness
and not to the Spirit of Light, their palaces were the
abodes of luxury and dissipation, and their cities of
crime and disorder. When they perished their cities
too were destroyed, and most of the mighty works they
had created crumbled to decay. Some few still remain
as monuments of their pride and fall; and the hunter
carried away by the chase, ofttimes comes suddenly
among them, and wonders what manner of men could
have piled up those huge blocks of hewn stone.

"Their name and their language are unknown, but
that they had learning far above the learning of the
men of the present day, and that they could read the
sun, and the moon, and the stars, and that they were
deeply versed in the mysteries of the universe, there is
no doubt. They still held communication with the
lands from whence they came, and brought thence
precious stones and fine cloths and spices, and valuables

of all sorts, to add to the beauty of their buildings,
the richness of their clothing, or the luxury of their
living. At length their science informed them that
there were regions towards the rising of the sun of
great wealth, inhabited by people small in stature, yet
of power equal to their own, so they longed to go and
take possession of their wealth, and to destroy the
people, lest they should grow more powerful than
themselves, and come and humble them. However,
this narrow portion of land intervened to separate the
ocean of the setting sun from the ocean of the rising
sun, and they were unable to build ships, such as those
in which they had come, nor did they know how to
convey them from one ocean to the other. At first
they thought of making a road over the land, but the
ships broke to pieces in the attempt; they next thought
of cutting a channel from one sea to the other, but
mountains and other impediments were in their way.
At last, while their chiefs and wise men were consulting on the subject, a fisherman who was out on the sea
in search of some of the monsters which then existed,
discovered a vast cavern in a black rock, horrid and
dreadful to the sight. He at once believed that it was
a fit temple to dedicate to the powers of darkness,
whom he worshipped; and when he came home, and
gave the account of what he had discovered, the neighbouring people flocked thither in numbers, and it has
ever since been called the Devil's Cave. Among others,
went some of the chiefs and wise men, and when they

D

saw the vast hollow in the rock, and that it reached
far under the land, they thought that, by means of the
art in which they excelled, it might be made to penetrate completely through the isthmus. So they called
all their cunning workmen together, and they began
the mighty undertaking. They blocked up the entrance of the Devil's Cavern down to the bottom of
the sea, and having emptied it of water, they hewed a
vast tunnel through the earth, which they arched with
huge blocks of stone, such as no workmen of the
present day could form.

"For two years they laboured at the work, and
triumphed in their pride at its success. In another
year they believed that they should open their tunnel
on to the eastern ocean, when, on a sudden, a loud
roaring noise was heard; the rock before them gave
way, a fierce tempest swept along the tunnel, the
waters of the ocean rushed through, and carried them,
and their tools, and the stones they had collected, far
out into the western sea. It was a punishment for their
impiety ; for they had attempted to penetrate into the
great Temple of the Sun, made at the commencement
of the world by no mortal hands.

"For ages that temple was never visited, till it was
discovered by our fathers in the days of their glory.
In those days they used to resort thither to worship ;
but when the white men came from the east and carried
them off captive, and destroyed their palaces and their
temples, they forgot that mighty temple, and the very

knowledge of its existence faded away from the memories of most men. A few only of the wise men knew of it, and it was recorded in their prophecies, that it should once again be discovered and once again lost; but that on the third discovery a new era of glory for this land should commence, and that the country should become covered with houses and fields, and that many people and large ships should come from the east, and should pass through it, and should carry their wealth even to the far west, and that there should be much traversing to and fro, and no longer poverty and misery in the land. The second discovery you have made; ages, perchance, may yet pass away before it is a third time discovered, for it would be ruin and destruction to us and to our children, if we were to show it to the white men, the cruel Spaniards; for they would come and carry us away captive to work for them, to build their cities and houses, to cultivate their fields, and to clear out this very tunnel. No, let us be wise—let us say nothing about it, and we may be safe."

"You are right, my aged friend," observed Hernan. "For my part I will say nothing about it, provided I can secure the treasure I beheld in the cavern. Nothing shall prevent my visiting the spot again."

"If you run the risk, you must take the consequences, my son," replied the sage. "The Cavern of the Sun has often been visited, and may be so again. It was the resort of some of your countrymen, who

came hither to avenge our wrongs on the Spaniards,
and to collect wealth for themselves, and this treasure
was a large portion of their booty which they were
unable to carry off. You are welcome to it, for to us
it is of no value. Of gold and silver we have abundance, if we chose to collect it, and jewels cannot give
us food, or houses, or clothing. Take, then, the treasure
and share it with your companions, and depart in peace
to your own land."

"I will do as you desire," answered Hernan. "And
now, cacique, I have another favour to ask. I love
your daughter, and I would take her with me as my
wife—a treasure I prize far more than the glittering
heaps now in the cavern."

The cacique, on hearing these words, turned his
glance on his daughter.

"How is this, Tara?" he said. "Have you bestowed your heart on this stranger? Speak, girl. If
you love him I will not thwart your wishes."

The Indian maiden looked at her parent and then at
Hernan.

"My love for you, my father, is deep and old, and
for your sake I am ready to die; that which I feel
for this stranger is new, and such as I cannot find
words to tell, but the new conquers the old. If you
forbid me not, I go where my heart leads me:" saying
this, she rose, and put her hand in that of Hernan.

Thus the pirate won his bride.

THE UNWELCOME STRANGERS.

The pirate Hernan stood on the rock overlooking the
bay, and Tara was by his side.   The schooner lay in
the centre of the harbour.   Her yards were squared, her
sails were bent, and she was ready for sea.   It was
towards evening, the rocks and lofty hills on the west
already cast their shadows over the water.   Not a
cloud dimmed the bright blue sky, and a light air,
which came up the gulf from the sea, just rippled its
surface with miniature waves, which fell with a gentle
murmur on the shore.

"It is our last evening, my Tara, in your native
land," said the pirate; "to-morrow we will secure

the treasure, and sail from hence to a country where your beauty will be prized, and where our riches will purchase lands, and titles, and all that men can desire. A glorious future, my loved one, is in store for us."

"I care not for titles or wealth, or aught else, so that I am with you," replied Tara. "I would willingly have passed my days here, with you by my side—but, ah! what is that white dot we see in the far distance, towards the entrance of the gulf?"

The pirate looked attentively in the direction towards which she pointed.

"It is the sails of a ship, as I live!" he exclaimed; "and those of another are visible too. There are three, and large ones, or I am mistaken. They may be friends, but we have few such, and my heart misgives me that they are enemies. Well, fortunately, we are ready for sea, and prepared to meet them, should they prove such; though three to one are fearful odds. Tara, we have no time to lose; we must at once on board, and get ready to receive them either as friends or foes. Our boat waits for us at the foot of the cliffs. I would leave you on shore, love, but we may be able to secure the treasure during the night, and pass these strangers in the dark, when the wind towards the morning comes off the land—at all events, we do not wish them to share the treasure."

He spoke as they were descending the cliff to the boat. A few minutes served to carry them to the side of the vessel, where loud cheers from the crew greeted their arrival.

"Welcome to our brave captain and his Indian bride," shouted the pirates. "He was bold before, he will be bolder still, now he has a wife to fight for. He has come to lead us on to victory and to wealth. Huzza—huzza—huzza!"

Louder and louder grew the cheers as they reached the deck, and the men pressed eagerly forward to catch a glance of the lovely countenance of their chief's young wife. He had long commanded them, and though stained by many a crime, he had gained their respect by his bravery and success, their love by his firmness and kindness. They were rough and ignorant, he was refined and educated, and he brought all his talents and sagacity into play to govern them. So well did he contrive to bend their wild spirits to his will, that they became virtually his slaves, and yet all the time they did not feel his yoke upon their necks.

"Thanks, my brave fellows," he exclaimed; "I know your love, and will try to merit it. And now I must tell you, that just as I left the shore, I saw three ships coming up the gulf; as the breeze is failing, they may not be off here till to-morrow morning; and, if they are, as I suspect, enemies, we must fight them, or manage to pass by them out to sea, without their perceiving us. However, in the meantime, I have an enterprise to which to lead you, which, if successful, will enrich us all. There is danger to be encountered, but from that I know none of you will shrink."

"What is it, captain? We are ready to follow wherever you lead," exclaimed a hundred voices.

"I felt sure you would," answered Hernan; and he gave an account of his adventures in the cavern, and explained briefly to them his intentions regarding the removal of the treasure, which afforded great satisfaction to his crew.

Having sent an officer on shore to watch the movements of the strangers, the captain set every one on board to work, to prepare the ship for action. It was a busy scene, such as Tara had never before witnessed. Some were employed in getting up powder and shot; some in sharpening cutlasses, and cleaning pistols and muskets; others loaded and ran out the guns; some, again, got the boats ready, or unmoored the ship. Meantime, the pirate officer who had been sent on shore climbed to the summit of the cliff, where he could watch the approach of the three strange sail. They came steadily, though slowly, up the centre of the gulf, and at last he was able to make them out to be three large ships, and from the cut of their sails, and their general appearance, he felt persuaded that they were Spanish men-of-war. The wind, however, failing them, they were compelled to anchor, when, the shades of night shutting them out from view, he hurried down to carry his information on board.

The news was received by the pirates without any feeling of dismay. They had so frequently and successfully encountered forces far superior to themselves, that, trusting to the talent of their leader, not a man had any doubt of the result on this occasion. Their greatest danger lay in being attacked during the night by the enemy's boats; for, with a good breeze, in their light, easily-manœuvred craft, they had little fear of being able to scrape by the three ships without much damage.

"Now, my men," exclaimed the captain, "the time has arrived to commence our enterprise, and in a few hours we shall have gold sufficient to make every one of us wealthy men for life."

At these words the crew cheered, the anchor was got up, the boats were sent ahead, and the schooner began slowly to move out towards the entrance of the cavern.

THE TREASURE GAINED.

There was no moon in the sky, neither did the stars shine forth to guide the pirates in their course, for a dense mist hung like a funeral pall over sea and land, and Hernan's superior skill and knowledge could alone have enabled them to venture on quitting their anchorage. No light could be made use of lest the Spaniards should see it, and none but seamen's eyes, long accustomed to work in darkness, could have perceived any object beyond the length of a man's arm. The sturdy crew, however, went about their duty as if it was broad daylight, and the men in the boats gave all their strength to towing out the vessel.

Hernan's intention was to take the schooner to the mouth of the cavern, then to go up in the boats to bring down the much-coveted treasure, and as soon as it was on board to make sail and to endeavour to pass by the Spaniards without observation. He laughed at the idea of their rage and disappointment when they found that he and his followers had completely eluded them.

It is extraordinary what discipline had been introduced among those rude men, and how readily they obeyed orders when they felt that obedience was necessary for the common good. Not a sound, consequently, was heard along the busy decks, except the low voices of the officers as they issued the requisite orders, and the gentle splash of the muffled oars as they dipped into the water. Hernan stood near the helmsman to direct him how to steer, and by his side was his faithful Tara, who never for a moment left this post. To her all was strange, new, and wonderful; she was not afraid, because he was with her, but she saw ample cause for alarm in the fierce looks of the men, their coarse voices, and strange language, though they were prepared to treat with due respect their captain's bride. The progress of the vessel was very slow, for not a breath of air was blowing from any quarter to fill her canvas, and the process of towing is very tedious—indeed, the risk of approaching that rocky shore under sail would have been very great, and even now there was some danger, though the lead was kept going from the headmost boat to give them warning in time of any sunken rock or sand-bank in their course. Look-outs, also, were stationed in every part of the vessel to watch for the approach of the enemy, should they have been enabled by any partial breeze to draw nearer to them.

The Indian girl watched all the proceedings in silence; but the manner in which the vessel was guided in her course astonished her most.

"How is it," at length she asked, "that you know in what direction to steer your ship towards the cavern, when that is far hid from your sight?"

"By this instrument—the mariner's faithful friend," he answered, showing her the binnacle, in which a burning light shed its rays on a compass; "the helmsman's eye is now intently fixed on it. One line always points to the north, the opposite to the south, and others to the rising and setting of the sun. Whatever way the vessel turns, so turns that point. Thus, when it was daylight, I marked well how the mouth of the cavern bore from hence by the compass just midway between the north and where the sun sets; and thus I know even in the darkest nights, by following the same line, that I shall reach the spot at which I aim. It is a wonderful invention, but there is nothing in it of magic, as you may perchance suppose; and before our voyage is over I shall have to show you many other things which will not the less surprise you."

"It is a world full of wonders," said the Indian girl, musing. "I feel that our very existence is wonderful. Tell me, Hernan, how soon can we hope to reach the beautiful land you speak of where you were born?"

"Many days, perhaps several moons, must pass away before we reach it," replied her husband.

"What! is the sea of so great an extent as that would signify?" she observed. "I wonder how men are found bold enough to venture on its trackless wilds."

"The thirst for wealth lures us on, my Tara—the restless spirit of adventure. The sea is the safeguard of our country; were it not for that, the fierce men who now seek on it an outlet for their unruly spirits would create disturbances and rebellions at home. It was fortunate for my country and myself that I had the ocean as my resource, or I should have proved a troublesome subject to my king."

Thus the pirate and his bride conversed as the vessel glided forward on her perilous expedition.

It must be understood that the schooner's course lay from one side of the gulf, the north shore, to its head or westernmost point, and thus that she was almost crossing the bows of the Spanish ships, if they remained where they had been seen at sunset. While the captain's attention was engaged in watching the course of the vessel, Tara's gaze was turned anxiously towards the east, where her eyes had been attracted by seeing what she took to be bright sparks, like fireflies, playing in the air. She pointed them out to Hernan, but his vision was not so acute as hers, and he thought she had been mistaken, for he observed nothing, and the circumstance was disregarded. For full an hour the pirates persevered in towing the vessel, for although in their boats they might have reached the mouth of the cavern in little more than half that time, yet Hernan was unwilling to leave the vessel in the presence of an enemy, without the whole strength of his crew on board, so long as would have been required to get the treasure and return. He thought, too, that a light breeze might possibly spring up and enable them to get up to the cavern under sail, which, notwithstanding the danger, was preferable to the slow mode of progress they were compelled to employ.

Every one on board was eager to feast his eyes on the promised treasure, and thus all were doubly anxious to spread their canvas to the wind. As the officers and men walked the deck, they spread the wet palms of their hands to every point of the compass to discover if one felt colder than another, but no difference for a long time was perceptible. At last a faint breeze, so slight that by no other means could it have been discovered, came over the land from the north; the topsails were let fall, the foresail was hauled out, and the mainsail hoisted, and the vessel slipped more easily than before through the water. The wind, however, soon died away; but after a little time it returned with greater force than before, and gaining further strength,

the boats were called on board, with the exception of
one, which proceeded ahead, to sound and give warning of danger.

It was a time of breathless interest, for the risk
was great. Every man was at his post, ready to clew
up the sails and bring the vessel, if necessary, to an
anchor. Each instant they expected to reach their
destination. Hernan now went to the fore part of the
vessel, to watch for the lofty cliffs by the side of the
cavern, if perchance they were to be distinguished
through the gloom. Notwithstanding the darkness, at
length he beheld them rising like a black wall to the
sky, and appearing ready, from their vast height, to
fall forward and overwhelm the vessel. The cliffs
were not so near as they seemed; the helm was kept
up, and the schooner, doubling the headland, stood
across into the very centre of the cavern's mouth. In
a minute the sails were furled, and the anchor was let
go, though the length of the cable which was required
showed the great depth of the water. There lay the
vessel under that mighty arch of rock, on one side the
comparatively clear expanse of sky and sea, on the
other a mass of impenetrable darkness—the veil which
shrouded the longed-for treasures. Dispositions were
now rapidly made for the expedition. Three boats,
with trusty crews, were to go. Hernan took the command in one, with two of his officers in the others.
The men were all armed and provided with torches.
The vessel was left under charge of the first-lieutenant,

while her guns were loaded and run out, and her men
prepared for action, or any emergency. Hernan would
have left Tara on board, but she insisted on accom-
panying him, and sharing all the dangers to which she
believed he would be exposed, either supernatural or
from being of mortal mould. She therefore sat by his
side as he steered the leading boat. Even the boldest
of the pirates entered on the expedition with awe and
doubt, and would have rather, by a hundred times,
engaged the three Spanish ships at once, or gone
through any other work, however hazardous, to which
they were accustomed in the light of day. But they
were not the men to flinch when their captain set them
an example. Hernan had had a compass placed in his
boat, by which he hoped to find his way up the wider
part of the cavern; but they had proceeded only a
short distance when he found that it varied so rapidly,
by some attractive influences in the cavern, that it
could not be depended on, and he was reluctantly compelled to order a torch to be lighted, though he was
afraid, by so doing, of alarming his people by the dreadful shapes with which he knew they were surrounded.
There was, however, no help for it, as it would be
impossible otherwise to find their way. A light was
struck, and in an instant a blazing torch illuminated
the gloom. If in the glorious light of the rising sun
the figures had appeared horridly fantastic, doubly
dreadful did they now seem in the flickering, uncertain
glare of the torch. A cry of terror escaped even the

stout hearts of the pirates as they looked up and beheld
directly above their heads, and frowning down on them
as if in anger at their intrusion, the monster of the
cavern, the mighty figure of the God of the Tempest,
and in the further distance shapes of all forms and
sizes just emerging from the gloom, one of which, of

hideous form, mounted on a charger as hideous as itself,
seemed about to descend upon them. Even Tara, who
had seen them before, shrank closer to the side of
Hernan for protection. He also, as he gazed at them,
could scarcely persuade himself that they were not
moving, as the glare of the torch played over them.
The head of the giant idol seemed to bend forward, his
eyes rolled, and his vast arm shook; the serpents which

lay in coils at his feet lifted up their heads, and appeared as if about to dart forward; the lions and tigers and other wild beasts seemed crouching down to spring on their prey, while every tower and minaret, every palace and church spire, castle wall or street of city, seemed to be glowing in the light of a distant conflagration.

Every feature of the wondrous scene was too flickering and uncertain to appear real, and each man, as he gazed, believed himself to be the victim of a delusion. The light did not penetrate as did that of the sun into the inner recesses of the cavern; indeed it was with difficulty that Hernan could count the entrance to each gallery so as to reckon their distance from the one which contained the treasure. The glare, however, reached as far as the schooner, which was discerned at the mouth of the cavern floating calmly on the dark water, the light just tinging her sides and her taper masts and spars, and showing the broad arch of the cavern overhead. As they beheld these strange sights, the pirates were about to pull back to the ship. It was some time, indeed, before they recovered from their astonishment and terror. Most of them believed it to be the work of enchantment, and expected every instant to find themselves in the grasp of the monster idol, or attacked by some of the ferocious beasts they saw in the distance. At last they were roused to exertion by the voice of their commander.

"What is it you are afraid of, my men?" he asked,

E

in an encouraging tone. "Do you think that the blocks
of stone you see around can be endued with life to injure us? I tell you I have passed them safely before,
and if you prove brave fellows, worthy of your former
selves, as I have known you, we shall again pass them
safely laden with wealth. If we go back now, like
dogs with their tails between their legs, we shall lose
our prize altogether, and have every chance of falling
into the tender hands of the Spaniards, who, let me
tell you, will run us up like hounds to their yard-arms
without mercy."

This speech had the desired effect. The men cheered,
and vowed that they were ready to face a whole legion
of devils, with Hernan at their head. As their voices
rose together, the roof and sides of the cavern echoed
with the sound, which reverberated into every gallery
and recess, till each strange monster seemed endued
with the power of speech as well as with life, and to
have joined their voices in one wild concert. The
noise rose and fell as it was carried along, often
varying in sound; and shrieks, and cries, and groans,
and shouts of mocking laughter burst forth, and were
heard proceeding from the furthest recesses of the
cavern.

The men now looked more aghast than before at
each other, and again Hernan had to exert his utmost
influence over them to induce them to proceed. Some,
indeed, seemed inclined to mutiny, and whispered
among themselves that their captain's Indian bride had

bewitched him, and would probably lead them all to destruction, and even proposed seizing her and throwing her overboard to preserve themselves. If their captain heard these mutterings, he did not notice them at the time, but he marked the traitor for a future day. So great, however, was his influence over the greater number from his uniform success, that notwithstanding their fears of the consequences, they continued to obey his orders, and once more bent stoutly to their oars. He encouraged them by laughing at their fears, by cheering them on, by describing the rich prize before them. As he spoke, his voice echoed along the galleries, and at length the men grew accustomed to the strange sounds and sights which had at first alarmed them. Hernan's boat took the lead, followed by the other two. Gallery after gallery was passed and counted carefully by him, but knowing the character of his followers, he did not deem it prudent to confide to any of them the secret of the method to find the spot where the treasure lay hid, and he was therefore the only person who counted the galleries. At length they drew near to the hundredth gallery, and even Hernan's heart beat quick at the expectation of becoming the possessor of so vast a store of wealth. The thought also occurred to him, that by some means or other it might after all prove deceptive.

Such are always the feelings which present themselves when some long-wished-for prize is almost within our grasp, to diminish the anticipated delight of possession—a faltering footstep, an accident of the most trivial nature, may deprive us of it for ever.

The boats dashed on at their utmost speed, their crews even laughing at the hideous shapes which started forth from their concealment as they advanced. On they went: the eightieth gallery was passed, the ninetieth was gained;—on they went: the hundredth was reached at last. With a voice thick with anxiety, Hernan ordered his men to lay in their oars and run the boats alongside the steps, an example followed by the others. More torches were now lighted, to enable them to avoid the numerous dark pits on either side of the gallery, and, Tara holding one hand, he led the way with a torch in the other. He advanced rapidly, but at the same time cautiously, for even he, much more his followers, almost expected every instant to be attacked by a legion of demons, or the spirits of the dead buccaneers, who were supposed to guard the hidden treasures collected by them in their lifetime. At last, so long a time had they been searching, that Hernan began to fear that they had missed it, or that it had disappeared altogether.

"Surely we were not so long before in reaching the treasure cavern," he observed to Tara; "we must almost be at the very end of the gallery—near the fathomless pit of which you spoke."

"Your eagerness deceives you," she replied: "a few paces more and we shall gain the spot we seek. See! there is the glittering heap; possess yourselves of

it, but be speedy, and let us begone, for something
tells me that danger is near, though I know not its
nature, nor whence it may come."

While she spoke she pointed to the entrance of a
large cavern, into which the glare of the torch pene-
trating exhibited the eagerly-sought pile of treasure.
As the pirates came up and beheld the tempting heap,
they showed the most extravagant signs of joy ;—some
danced and sung, others rolled themselves among the
scattered jewels and coin, while others loaded every
part of their persons with such of the treasure as they
could stow away. It was some time before Hernan
could restrain them and bring them back to their
senses, urged all the time to hurry on the work by
Tara, who gazed with feelings of contempt and pity on
what she considered the madness of his followers. He
at last induced them to fill the sacks and baskets they
had brought, and each man carrying as much as his
strength would allow, they returned to the boats.
Having emptied the precious contents into the bottom
of the boats, they insisted on returning for more,
although already somewhat heavily laden, and urged
by Tara to retreat at once. Even Hernan, who had
been persuaded by her of the danger they ran, was
disobeyed, and men hurried back with shouts and cries
of joy to get more of the treasure. All their fears of
demons, or the spirits of dead pirates, were forgotten
—for gold alone they thought or cared. Again the
cavern was reached, and every bag and basket filled;

but the glittering heap seemed in no way diminished. Staggering under the weight of their loads they returned at last, and emptied the contents into the boats, when even they perceived that they could hold no more. Indeed, by the time they had taken their seats, the boats were sunk almost to their gunnels in the water. Hernan then gave the word to shove off, and pulling into the centre of the main channel, he turned the head of his boat in the direction from whence they had come. Tara, whose fears for their safety had increased, reminded him of the whirlpool into which they had before got, and which, by the turns it had caused them to make, had sent them completely through the tunnel; but he quelled her alarm, by assuring her that with light to guide them they could mark the side of the cavern, and easily keep on their right course. Their return was slower than their coming, for not only were the boats laden deeply, but the men were fatigued with their exertions.

They were all in high spirits, and were laughing and joking at their former fears, when just as they had performed about three-quarters of the distance, a loud rattling sound assailed their ears, echoing and reverberating throughout the vast cavern;—again and again it was repeated, till it seemed as if a whole army was engaged in combat.

" It is musketry!" exclaimed Hernan. " Give way, my men—give way; depend on it the Spaniards have attacked the schooner."

The pirates strained at their oars till the stout ash
sticks almost bent double with their exertions.   Still
they would not heave overboard any of their precious
cargo, though urged to do so by Tara; and, laden
as they were, their progress was comparatively slow.
However, there was no need to encourage them to

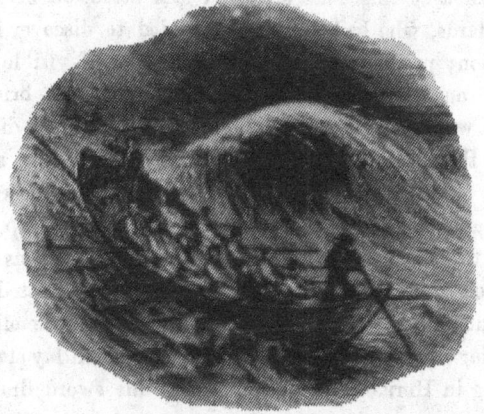

exertion, for every man was eager to be engaged with
the enemy in defence of the schooner, if, indeed, she
were attacked.   Of this they had no doubt by the time
they reached the giant statue, when they beheld the
bright flashes of guns illuminating the mouth of the
cavern, and even heard the very clashing of the swords
of the combatants—a proof that they had come to
close quarters.   On finding this, the eagerness of the
pirates increased, and they would have shouted out in
their excitement: but Hernan warned them not to

cheer, so as not to give the enemy notice of their
approach.   From musketry alone being heard, and
the clash of steel, it was clear that the Spanish ships
had not come up, but that the enemy had attacked the
schooner with their boats, and Hernan recollecting
the bright glare produced by the torches, felt convinced that this had attracted the attention of the
Spaniards, who had thus been enabled to discover her
position; probably, indeed, she was herself visible to
those on board the Spanish ships while the bright
light was glowing behind her.   As the pirates drew
near their schooner they could hear the shouts and
cries of the combatants, and dashing on, they were
soon alongside, and the most daring scrambled up on
deck to join in the fray, while the more cautious remained to hand up the treasure they had collected at
so much risk.   The sound of battle and the smell of
powder awakened all the fierce passions which lay slum-
bering in Hernan's bosom, and with his sword drawn
he sprang on deck, where the enemy had just gained a
footing.   Tara followed him closely, not even waiting
for his assistance; nor would she listen to his hurried
entreaties and commands to go below to be out of
danger.

"What should I be afraid of when I am near
you?" she answered.   "Where you are, there will I
be also."

The schooner lay with her broadside open to the
mouth of the cavern, and the Spaniards had only

ventured to attack her on the outer side and on the bows, which circumstance had enabled the diminished crew of the pirates to keep them at bay much longer than they could otherwise have done; indeed, such a style of fighting was not at all suited to the taste of the Dons. It was a scene of wild confusion in which Hernan found himself, lighted up occasionally by the flashes of the pistols, or as the thickly padded garments of the Spaniards caught fire from the wadding of the guns. On one side of the vessel were seen the boats of the enemy, eight or ten in number, some at a distance, disabled from the shot thrown into them; others still alongside, the crews of which were trying to get on board, and were hotly engaged with the pirates, giving and receiving thrusts from long pikes; while others, more daring, were fighting hand to hand, clinging on to the rigging or the nettings, and just within the bulwarks. Those who had got thus far discovered the weakness of the pirate crew, and were encouraging their countrymen to renew the attack with greater vigour.

Such was the state of affairs when Hernan with his men threw himself on the deck, and though fatigued with their long pull they yet felt fresh for the combat. With loud shrieks and cries they rushed at the enemy. The tide of battle was again completely turned. The Spaniards who had gained the deck were cut down without mercy; those on the rigging or the nettings were hurled into the sea or cast into the

boats alongside; and the boats themselves were either
sunk by the heavy shot thrown into them, or driven to
a distance by the hot fire which assailed them; while
the loud cheers of the pirates showed them that they
had little chance of success by a second attack. After
firing a few ineffectual shots, they were seen by the
flashes of those which the pirates returned to collect
together, and to steer directly down the centre of the
bay, in the direction where the ships were supposed to
lie.   It was extraordinary to see the effect of the
flashes from the fire-arms, for every time one was discharged, the wild strange figures in the distant parts of
the cavern appeared as if starting forth, and again
retiring as the light died away. Hernan's first care
was for Tara. She was uninjured, but alarmed at the
scene she had witnessed; yet he had great difficulty in
persuading her to retire to her cabin to take the rest she
so much required. His next care was to secure the
treasure which was now piled up in heaps on the deck.
Such of the pirates who now for the first time saw it
by the light of a torch, which made the jewels and
gold sparkle brilliantly, gave way to the most extravagant signs of joy, as their shipmates had done before
them; and when they heard that there was still more
to be got from whence that came, they insisted on
going to fetch it. Hernan said all he could to dissuade
them; but though his orders were implicitly obeyed in
times of danger or in action, on an occasion of this sort
he was powerless to curb their inclinations.

"My men," he exclaimed, "you have already collected as much wealth as you can possibly know how to spend; and if you return for more, you will run into many dangers from which no bravery can save you. Follow my advice. Let us get under weigh at once, and while the Dons are in confusion and in a violent rage from the drubbing we gave them, let us slip past and put the mouth of the gulf between them and us. Once in the open sea, we can show them a clean pair of heels, and get safe off with our treasure. With that on board, we have nothing more to do with fighting if we can help it."

"We have not got enough by half," shouted several voices; "why should we leave so much bright gold to the rascally Spaniards, or to any other fellows, when we might with a little trouble go and get it? The gold we must and will have—so, hurrah, my boys! who'll man the boats to go for it?"

"Stay!" shouted Hernan, when he found the men jumping into the boats, and saw that no argument would restrain them. "By yourselves you cannot find the treasure, and would to a certainty lose your lives; and no one shall say that I, your captain, deserted you. I will go with you; but you must promise me not to overload the boats, and to hasten back as fast as possible."

"Huzza for our brave captain!" exclaimed the crew. "He is the man to lead us on all occasions. Huzza! huzza!"

Before Hernan left the schooner he entered the cabin. Tara lay on her couch wrapped in a deep slumber, occasioned by her exertions and the anxiety to which she had been subject. He gazed at her fondly.

" I will not awake you," he muttered; " you may sleep on securely in your innocence, for the great God whose laws I have outraged, but whom you have never wontonly offended, will send his guardian angels to watch over you and protect you. Farewell, my precious one! I will return ere you awake, and you may be spared the fears my absence would cause you, did you know of it."

He kissed her smooth brow. She smiled, but did not awake ; and he hurried from the cabin.

Some hours passed away before Tara awoke. A small silver lamp burnt in the cabin, and shed its pale light around. She rose, in expectation of finding Hernan present. He was not there. She called on his name, but he did not answer. Throwing her mantle around her she went on deck in search of him, and great was her grief and alarm when she found that he had quitted the ship without informing her of his intention, and had not returned. She at once concluded that he had gone in search of further treasure, and she anxiously endeavoured to penetrate the gloom of the cavern to discover if the boats were returning; but not a glimmering of light could be seen, and in vain did her ears listen for the sound of the oars of his boat in the water. Poor girl! no one could understand her inquiries or comprehend her fears. The

officer left in command, however, had begun to be
rather anxious for Hernan's return, as he thought that
it was now high time that they should be getting under
weigh, if they were to endeavour to give the Spaniards
the slip before the night was over. Yet, as he was
not a man given to loquacity, and as he knew that by
talking about it he would not come more speedily, he
continued his silent and solitary walk on the quarter-
deck. A few other men were following his example;
while the remainder of the watch on deck were keeping a bright look-out from their stations in different
parts of the ship. The rest of the crew were
below, snatching a short repose, with their arms
by their sides, to be ready to repel another attack.
Tara had perfect faith in Hernan, for love cannot
exist without it; but she felt that it would have been
more considerate of him to have told her if he must go,
and much wiser in him to have quitted without delay
so dangerous a locality. As she valued little the
treasure which had tempted the pirates to run so great
a risk, so did she think lightly of the temptation which
had induced them to go. With hurried steps, and a
heart sinking with apprehension, she continued to pace
the deck; for though weary in body and mind, she
could not return to the cabin, the air of which appeared
to her hot and suffocating. The time wore on, and the
expedition did not return. Even the men at length
began to be alarmed; but their fears were more for
themselves, lest the Spaniards should come upon them

and destroy them while they were thus short-handed, and they should lose all the treasure they had collected. Still the boats did not return. Although, looking towards the interior of the cavern, all appeared of darkest gloom, yet, seaward, a faint light streak already ushered in the dawn. With increased fears Tara beheld it grow broader and brighter, knowing that in a short time the schooner would be full in view of their overpowering enemy.

Gradually the shades of night withdrew, and the silvery light of the early morn came on, while the streak in the east widened and assumed a yellow, then an orange, and lastly a ruddy hue, while the three Spanish ships were seen emerging from the darkness, their masts and spars and the tracery of their rigging becoming well defined and marked against the clear sky.

When they found themselves in this dangerous position, the pirates were undecided what to do. Some proposed to leave their comrades to their fate, and endeavour to run past the Spaniards even in daylight, which, should there spring up a breeze, in their easily-worked vessel they might possibly accomplish; others were for remaining where they were; some thought of escaping with their booty to the shore; and the rest were for running the schooner further up the cavern, and defying the pursuit of the enemy. The opinion of the second-named party prevailed, and it was determined to make everything ready for action, to get a spring on their cable, and to wait the return of the boats where they were. Tara watched these preparations with intense interest. The movements of the crew were quickened by their observing the topsails of the Spanish ships let fall, and their anchors run up to the bows. Sail after sail was then set on them till they presented wide fields of white canvas spread out against the ruddy sky, though as yet the sails hung uselessly against the masts.

The Spaniards, however, probably observed the coming breeze in the distance, though it was hid from the eyes of the pirates. At last the lighter sails were seen to bulge out, the others soon became also filled with the wind, and the vast fabrics glided forward. On they came, in their glory and their pride, like three mighty giants, to perform their work of destruction. Even the sturdy pirates saw them approach with dismay, for with their enfeebled crew they could not hope successfully to contend with them; but still, encouraged by their officers, they went about their duties with alacrity and steady silence, which proved their determination. Tara gazed with increased anxiety up the cavern—but no boats or lights were to be seen. Was it fancy? Could she hear the fall of oars in the water? She listened with still greater attention, and was certain that she was not mistaken.

" They come, they come ! " she exclaimed, pointing eagerly up the cavern with an expression of joy.

The pirates did not understand her language, but conjectured by her gestures that she fancied the boats were returning. As she spoke, a yellow hue began to pervade the cavern, the upper extremities of the vast stalactites becoming tinged apparently with gold. Gradually the aureate tints extended throughout each stalactite, one catching the reflection of the other, till the whole roof, lately a dark arch, became like a canopy of burnished gold. Towards the ocean the sun was seen just rising above the calm waters, and as he seemed to float for an instant on its bosom before he began his upward course, his rays penetrated into the inmost recesses of the cavern, and it was then, in that glorious blaze of light, that the boats were perceived rapidly approaching the schooner. On they came, as fast as their crews could bend their backs to the oars. At the same time the Spanish ships, which had been gradually nearing the mouth of the cavern, were seen to take in their lighter sails, and to make preparations for rounding to, so as to bring their broadsides to bear upon the schooner. Tara's heart bounded with joy as she once more beheld Hernan returning in safety. She thought not, and cared not, for the danger to which they were exposed, for it was to be shared with him she loved.

Nearer and nearer the ships approached, till it was doubtful whether the boats could get alongside the schooner before they would open their fire. The pirates cheered lustily as they saw their comrades drawing close to them. It seemed as a signal for the ships to commence their work of destruction; for scarcely had the sound of human voices died away among the recesses of the cavern than the loud roaring report of a cannon was heard, followed by others in rapid succession, which echoed in loud thunders from rock to rock till the din became almost deafening, and its sound was as if two mighty fleets were engaged in battle. The pirates, in return, commenced firing; but the ships were at too great a distance from the schooner for their shot to tell with any effect. On seeing this, the Spaniards again kept away and stood on towards the cavern. They had been deceived in the distance by the well-defined outline of the schooner, as her dark hull appeared amid the blaze of light which surrounded her. Tara saw not what was going forward. She heard not the noise, and saw not the shot as they bounded into the cavern; for her whole being was concentrated on the rapidly approaching boats. A few more strokes, and they will be on board. "Huzza, huzza, huzza!" again the men cheered. The boats ran alongside, and the first who sprang on deck was Hernan. With a cry of joy, Tara threw herself into his arms. He returned her caress affectionately; and then, disengaging himself, he gave orders to get the schooner under weigh. There was by that time a light air blowing directly up the mouth of the cavern.

"This is no place for us to remain in," he exclaimed; "the enemy will blow us completely out of the water if we stay where we are. When we get sail on the vessel, we must retreat up the cavern, where, if they follow, they must take the consequences."

F

While sail was being made on the schooner and the anchor hove up, some of the men were engaged in unloading the boats, which were more full than ever of treasure. The schooner had just got under weigh, when the three ships again hauled up, and let fly their broadsides directly into the cavern, the shot falling into the calm water near her, or rattling and bounding against the rocks, but without striking her.

"Now," shouted Hernan to his men, as the schooner's broadside was still turned to the ships, "fire, my men, and remember that none of your shot miss."

The crew obeyed ; and their fire seemed to have some effect, for several of the enemy's spars were seen to tumble down on deck. This evidently enraged them, for they immediately again filled their sails and stood on, to be closer in to the mouth of the cavern. The schooner, instead of waiting to receive them, also kept away, and under Hernan's guidance ran directly up the centre of the cavern. Tara still hung on Hernan's arm.

"Fear not," he said ; "we can run the vessel up one of the numerous galleries at hand if we are hard pressed, and the enemy will never find us."

As the schooner led, the ships followed so eagerly in the pursuit, that, before they were aware of it, they got completely under the arch of the cavern, holding, indeed, the same position that the schooner had during the night. Finding that it was too late to retreat—for, as the wind was blowing directly into the cavern, they could not work out again—and as they were afraid of proceeding further, they let go their anchors and furled their sails, probably intending to destroy the pirates before they attempted to tow out the ships— the only means by which they could hope to retrace their path. Thus, at all events, all hope of escape in that direction was cut off, and no one but Hernan and Tara yet knew of the passage under the isthmus. The pirate crew beheld these arrangements with no little apprehension, for even the dullest saw that if the vessel was not sunk, they should probably be starved out, as two of the enemy's ships could keep guard while the other went in search of provisions. They appeared, then, to be caught in a trap. Hernan, however, calmed their alarm, and promised them the victory.

"To show them that we despise them, we will this time be the first to commence the action," he exclaimed. "Fire, my men; fire steadily, and low."

Scarcely had he spoken, when several shots were seen to take effect on the hulls of the enemy's ships, the white splinters glancing off in every direction. This increased the rage of the Spaniards, who, bringing their broadsides to bear on the schooner, discharged their whole batteries at her. Just then the shield of the Spirit of the Storm sent forth a ray of dazzling splendour.

"Alas!" exclaimed Tara, "this bloody strife is a profanation of the temple of the divinity, and he will not fail to avenge himself on our heads."

She spoke as the thunder of the enemy's guns was heard, and the shot came rattling about the ship, and tearing off huge pieces of stalactite from the sides of the cavern.

The light which had before pervaded the cavern was far brighter than that of the open air, and now the whole interior became as it had appeared when Hernan and Tara first visited it, filled with an atmosphere of a bright golden hue, dazzling to the sight, so that objects were less clearly distinguishable than when the light was less intense. This circumstance probably prevented the Spaniards from taking so good an aim as they would otherwise have done. The action now began in earnest. The Spaniards continued firing as rapidly as they could load, their shot flying in all directions, and reaching often into the far recesses of the cavern; some even struck the gigantic idol, but without making much impression; but few inflicted any serious injury on the schooner. Now and then one would come tearing across her decks, or wounding her spars and rigging, and several men were struck down, and sent to their last account; but this only increased the rage of the survivors, who worked their guns with still greater alacrity, careless of the shot and the spars and blocks which came tumbling down on their heads. A still greater danger, indeed, threatened them, from the masses of stalactite which, either struck off by the cannon-balls or shaken by the concussion, fell from the roof in all directions, appearing like meteors in their

rapid descent into the water. Fortunately, none fell
actually on to the deck of the schooner, or she might
have been sent to the bottom.

The schooner lay with her fore-topsail to the mast,
ready to move in any direction which might be considered necessary, while the ships had their anchors
down to prevent their drifting further in, and were
thus unable, on any sudden emergency, to shift their
position. The smoke also from the guns rose in dense
masses, and, spreading throughout the cavern, gradually obscured the atmosphere; and so thick did it
become, that it was only as the light breeze, which
still came in from the ocean, cleared it away, that the
combatants could at length see each other.

Hernan had again entreated Tara to go below, but
no argument or prayers could induce her to quit his
side; yet even her courage nearly gave way, as the
terrific din, and the scene of havoc, destruction, and
carnage increased.

Wherever he went she followed, as he flew from gun
to gun to encourage his men, and to see that they aimed
with precision.

"Oh, let us fly while there is yet time," she exclaimed; "depend on it, the outraged deity of the
cavern will avenge himself on our heads, and we and
the enemy shall be overwhelmed in a universal ruin.
We may escape in the boats up the cavern, where the
Spaniards will not dare to follow us, or, if they do,
we may lay concealed in one of the many caverns,

while they in vain search for us. If you would save our lives and that of the crew, do not neglect my advice."

"I would, for your sake, my Tara, do all you desire," answered Hernan; "but we pirates are sworn not to desert our ship while she remains afloat; and even now we are a match for the enemy, and injure them more than they hurt us. If they do not attempt again to attack us in their boats, which I do not think they will, we may even now gain the victory, and be able to sail out of the cavern in spite of those proud ships which now block up the entrance."

"I wish that I had hopes that we might so escape!" she replied; "but ah, see! the very roof of the cavern seems to tremble, and the Spirit of the Tempest shakes his head in anger—see! see!"

As she spoke she pointed upwards, and her voice could no longer be heard amid the loud roaring of the guns repeated by a thousand echoes, the shrieks and the shouts of the men, and the rattling of the falling stalactites. To add to the horrors of the scene, a dark shadow was seen descending from the roof and gradually filling the cavern, the obscurity being increased by the clouds of smoke from the guns of the combatants. Although these phenomena must have alarmed the Spaniards, they still perseveringly fought their ships. For a short time their fire slackened; but they were concentrating their strength for a greater effort; and having allowed the smoke to blow off, and loaded all their guns, at a given signal the three ships discharged them at once in the hopes of sinking the schooner. Louder than ever and more terrific was the roar, as the shot came flying over and about the pirate ship, piercing her hull and killing and wounding many of her people. She reeled with the shock, and Hernan felt that another such discharge would prove his last. But far more fatal to the Spaniards was the effect of these broadsides, for the vast arch of the cavern, previously shaken by the concussion, now trembled violently, as if upheaved by an earthquake; rock after rock gave way, and further loosened the remainder. The crews of the Spanish ships beheld with despair their coming fate, from which they had no human means of escape. "To the boats! to the boats!" was the horror-stricken cry. The guns were deserted, and the men rushed to lower their boats in the attempt to escape; but it was too late. Down came the ponderous mass with a crash which surpassed the roar of the artillery in loudness. In an instant the hapless ships were overwhelmed, crushed, and driven down bodily beneath the water, as if they had been mere withered leaves floating on its surface—not a human being of all those who lately peopled their decks escaped. Still the rocks and huge masses of earth continued to rush down, blackening the air in their fall and blocking up the entrance. Rapidly as words can utter it, a reef of rocks rose above the water, and the ruin still proceeding, a complete wall was formed, which blocked up the magic cavern from

the light of day or the further ingress of man. Such
was the summary manner in which the Spirit of the
Tempest appeared to avenge himself on the heads of
those who, without making a propitiatory offering, had
audaciously ventured within the precincts of his temple.

But what had become of the pirate-schooner while
this tremendous event was taking place? Was destruction also to overtake her?

When Hernan perceived that the enemy had ceased
firing, he, guessing the reason, saw that the best way
to escape from the iron shower from which his vessel
had already suffered so severely, was to run further up
the cavern; and, accordingly, there being still light
sufficient for him to steer by, he ordered the helm to
be put up, and filling the topsail, he boldly kept up
the cavern. Before the final catastrophe occurred the
schooner had run some way up, and as by the lead the
water was found of great depth, he had hopes of effectually evading the enemy. At last the broadsides of
the enemy sent forth their dying showers; but as the
schooner presented but a small mark, few of the shots
hit her, and though some of her men were killed, her
hull was uninjured. The echoes of the discharge, followed by those of the crash of the falling arch, filled
the cavern with a deafening din, more frightful than
any which had before been heard. The water rose in
wild waves, and almost dashed the schooner against the
sides; and as the noise continued, the atmosphere became close and oppressive, and a thick darkness filled

the cavern. Hernan saw it coming on, and had torches lighted in time, or nothing could have preserved the schooner from destruction. For some time the schooner continued rocking to and fro; and had she not, by the skilful guidance of Hernan, been kept in the centre of the channel, where the wind rushing through the upper part of the cavern, which still remained open, enabled him to hold steerage way on her, she must, even there, have been lost. His men, indeed, as it was, gave way to despair when they saw the entrance of the cavern blocked up, and fully believed that they were consigned to a lingering death within this mighty sepulchre.

Hitherto they had been in all respects obedient; but now, seeing, as they thought, a fearful fate staring them in the face, some went below, intending to break into the spirit-room, and others came tumultuously aft, where Hernan, with Tara by his side, was standing near the helm, and with fearful imprecations accused him of carelessly leading them to destruction.

"Why did you tempt us to come here after the devil's gold?" they exclaimed. "By this time the chances are it is turned into copper, and the jewels into sand. Now you have got us into this precious trap, can you, or that little Indian witch there, help us out again?"

Some spoke, while the rest used threatening gestures, and those who held the torches waved them wildly around, the red glare falling on the glittering sides and roof of the lofty cavern, on the sails of the vessel, and along the surface of the agitated water; while it gave to their own enraged and terror-stricken countenances an almost demoniacal expression. Hernan regarded them for a minute with proud contempt, while his heart swelled with indignation.

"Cowards!" he exclaimed—"and I am sorry to call men who have often fought so bravely by that name—you accuse me of thoughtlessly leading you to destruction, and of mocking you with false treasure by the aid of witchcraft. Now, I answer you, without me you would have long since been in the power of your enemies; and had I chosen it, I might have made the rich store of wealth with which our vessel is laden my own, without inviting you to share it; but I adhered to our laws, and you seem inclined to break them. However, I pardon you. Return to your duty; and as I have hitherto led you on all occasions to success, I now promise you that, if you obey my orders, I will carry you safely out of this difficulty."

This dauntless and confident speech completely curbed the fierce passions of the pirates, and calmed their fears, though many looked up with a longing glance at the small speck of blue sky which was seen through the remaining opening of the cavern, in the intervals between each fresh avalanche of rocks which came rushing down to fill it up.

"To your stations, my men, and we will make more sail on the schooner," continued their captain; and the crew obeyed his orders, although it appeared to them

that the vessel was rushing on into eternal night, or
rather into the very bowels of the earth. As they
proceeded the waves gradually subsided, and the
schooner held her tranquil course along the immense
cavern. Had it not been, however, for the reflective
power of the stalactites, which threw the lights always
a considerable distance ahead, they could not have
been able to see their way. The wind still blew along
the cavern in their favour, and a current also ran in
the same direction, so that their progress was rapid
indeed; had there been any sunken rocks in the way
they could scarcely have avoided striking on them.
When they got to the mouth of the cave containing
the remainder of the treasure, avarice getting the better
of the fears of some of the men, they wished to bring
the vessel to an anchor while they could get it on
board; but to this Hernan would not consent, assuring
them that the danger was great, and that they had
already more wealth than any of them would know
what to do with. As the discussion was going forward
they ran past the gallery, when the more sensible of
the crew siding with the captain, the rest were silenced.
The schooner soon afterwards came before the entrance
of the artificial tunnel; and great was the surprise of
all, except Hernan and Tara, when they found themselves beneath its solid roof of masonry. The water
was here much shallower, in consequence probably of
the masses of rock which gave way as the workmen
broke into the Temple of the Sun, and which the

current had not yet carried off; but the schooner fortunately glided through them unhurt, and continued her subterranean course. Hour after hour passed away, and the crew stood at their stations mute with astonishment and admiration at their captain's knowledge, for he wisely had not informed them of where they were going, and little did any of them suppose that they were sailing directly under the isthmus. Their progress was, of course, much slower than had been that of the canoe on Hernan's first voyage; and after some time the breeze died completely away, and they were compelled to tow the schooner along. Thus, not only the whole day, but the whole night was consumed before they reached the outlet. So easily, indeed, did they proceed, that one watch went to their berths below as if they had been in the open sea. It was soon after the period when, by their timepieces, it should have been morning, that the look-out forward exclaimed that he saw the light of day in the far distance, and the people eagerly crowded forward to behold what they never expected again to see. Continuing on some time further, Hernan ordered the torches to be extinguished, and to the joy of all, bright daylight burst upon their sight.

They were just then emerging from the tunnel into the Devil's Cave. The pirates cheered loudly, and the crews of the boats towing ahead pulled lustily as they once more glided over the heaving water of the ocean, though they were still under the black arch of the cavern. Still greater was their joy as they cleared it altogether; and a light air from the north filling their sails, the boats were called alongside, and they found themselves once more beneath the blue canopy of heaven. They now clustered round their chief, and by every means in their power expressed their satisfaction and gratitude.

"Huzza, for our noble captain!" they shouted; "huzza for the leader who has filled our pockets with gold! Huzza, huzza!'

The breeze freshened; every inch of sail the vessel could carry was set, and onward she bounded, boldly and free, over the bosom of the wide ocean.

The *Serpent* held her course towards the southern points of America's mighty continent. The crew were not a little disappointed when they found that they had a long voyage before them round Cape Horn, instead of the short passage across the Atlantic; but Hernan reconciled them to the delay by reminding them that they should have had to run the gauntlet through a number of vessels which were on the look-out for them, whereas that now they should be able to reach Europe without molestation, and might land their wealth at some quiet port, without much risk of suspicion. The *Serpent* had the damages she had received in the action with the Spaniards speedily repaired at an uninhabited island in the Pacific, which Hernan had selected from there being there no temptation to induce his men to spend their wealth, which, with the thoughtlessness of seamen, they would most certainly have done had they enjoyed the opportunity. On sailed the pirate-ship, the richest argosy which was floating on the bosom of the deep.

But was the chief owner of that wealth happy? He thought himself so. He possessed everything in anticipation which man could wish for; gold in abundance, health, and strength, an appearance which all must admire, and, more than all, a bride whom he devotedly loved. Day after day that love had increased; day after day her beauty seemed more refined and perfect; and, as her mind expanded under his persevering efforts to teach her the language, and the lore—and, strange as it may seem, the religion, too, of England—new beauties were every day developed. She was, in truth, the sunny spot in his existence. When his eyes were fixed on her he thought not of his former crimes; conscience slumbered, and he was at peace. Since he had known her he had ceased from committing fresh crimes, and he fancied himself a reformed man.

Tara was all life and animation—a new existence was opening to the comprehension of the Indian girl. For the first time she learnt the extent of the globe, the history of mankind, the various races of the human species, the varieties of the animal kingdom, the phenomena of nature; her mind was filled with wonder and delight; words could not express her pleasure, all was so new and beautiful. Thus did the once fierce pirate pass his time. No longer were the wealthy settlements they passed examined to discover whether they might venture on an attack, and the merchant-ships of all nations were allowed to sail by unmolested, Hernan's only public care being to guide the ship by the most direct course, and to keep the crew from quarrelling among themselves.

The *Serpent* had passed the western coast of America, and was attempting to double that stormy point, Cape Horn, when, being driven far to the south, she became entangled among lofty icebergs, which threatened her with destruction. A fierce gale also arose, with sleet, and snow, and cold, which continued for many days, when the presence of Hernan was required constantly on deck to preserve the ship from destruction. Thither Tara invariably accompanied him fearless of all danger, to behold those floating islands of ice and snow so new to her sight, and to watch the lofty waves, the forked lightning, and the fast-driving clouds. She, the child of a genial clime, was then exposed to cold her frame was unprepared to bear.

The storm abated, the ship was uninjured, and once more proceeded gaily on her course. Again they entered a warmer clime; but a change was taking place in Tara, though Hernan did not perceive it. Her spirits became uncertain, though at times higher than ever; her cheek grew thinner and paler, though at times the colour came in a clear spot which mocked the hue of health; yet her bright eyes were brighter than before, and beamed with a love as deep as ever on Hernan. At length, too, her strength failed, and she could no longer attend to the studies in which Hernan delighted to instruct her. Still the sad truth had not broken on his mind. The blow was to come with more awful and sudden effect.

It was a beautiful evening; a soft air from the south wafted the ship gently over the glassy deep. The sun was setting in splendour over Tara's distant land, as she lay propped up with cushions on the deck, where she had expressed a wish to be carried to enjoy the pure atmosphere of Heaven. Hernan knelt by her side, his hand in hers.

"The crisis of your illness has passed, my love," he said; "you will soon recover; and by the time we reach the shores of England you will be able to enjoy the homage and luxury, and the delight which rank and wealth can secure for us. A short time only is to be passed, and all we wish for can be ours."

"Hernan," she whispered, "I must not mock you with vain hopes;—a warning I cannot doubt tells me they are vain. Could aught retain my spirit on earth, it would have been my love for you; but an irresistible power calls me away. Still will I return and hover o'er you. The thought that I must quit you kills me. Hernan, my own—I die."

The stern pirates wept when they found that that beautiful creature was dead. They bore their captain senseless to his cabin; and he spoke not to any one till the *Serpent* was off a British port. Then his oath and his duty to his men called him into action.

The pirate's treasure was safely landed. Hernan's share bought him lands and titles, and again he assumed the name he once had borne; but nought brought back joy to his heart; for his bride, the only being he had ever loved, slept in her ocean grave.

G

BILLY COMBE'S LAST FIGHT:

A TRUE TALE OF THE HAMPSHIRE COAST.

BILLY COMBE was as bold and dashing a fellow, as gay and handsome, as fearless and as careless, as ever wore a pig-tail, or chewed tobacco. He figured upon the earth and sea, for on either element he was equally at home, somewhere about sixty years ago, more or less. There is no necessity to be very exact about dates.

The less we say about Billy Combe's moral character, perhaps the better, for though he considered himself the very pink of correctness when judged by his own code of morality, it must be acknowledged by his warmest admirers, that the said code was a very lax one, according to the notions generally held by the stricter portions of society at the present day. Billy argued that if no laws existed, there could be no crime; and that of all laws, strict revenue laws and high duties being most detrimental to the state, he not only did not feel himself called upon to subscribe to them, but to oppose them to the utmost of his power. This he did most effectually —in truth, he was one of the most daring and successful smugglers on the coast of Hampshire.

If Billy Combe had, like other men, his faults and failings, he had, which is all that can be said for the best of us, his good qualities also. He was generous in the extreme; he never turned a beggar away with a surly frown and without a groat, and while he had a shot in the locker it was at the service of a shipmate. His word was as good as his bond, which is as much as the proudest merchant can say; in some cases, among that class, one is worth as much as the other, namely nothing; but Billy's word was never broken, and of bonds he knew nothing. Staunch to his friends, and to those who put confidence in his honour, he would rather have died like the Indian at the fiery stake than have betrayed one who trusted him. Honest in all his dealings, when he made a bargain it was a fair one,

He would have disdained to take advantage of another man's embarrassments, and scorned the thought of *doing* any one.

" Oh, ye high and mighty ones, ye wealthy merchants revelling in luxury, ye lawyers with your flowing wigs, ye doctors with your long faces, ye jockeys whose conversation is of horse-flesh, ye rulers of the land, foreign ministers, home ministers, and would-be ministers, can ye say as much for yourselves ? "

Thus used Billy occasionally to exclaim when, during his moments of relaxation, with pipe in his mouth, he indulged, like other great heroes, in the pleasure of boasting of himself and his deeds.

The only people he *did* were the revenue officers, and them he *did* with a vengeance; but at the same time, he considered such *doing* all fair and above board.

He acknowledged himself to be a smuggler; he never concealed the fact from any one; he gloried in smuggling, it was his profession, his business, his delight, his amusement; he gave full notice that he should smuggle on to the end of his days, or till the revenue laws were abolished, and even in that respect he kept his word. They might catch him if they could, but that was not so easy a matter. If caught, he was ready to undergo the penalty

This once happened. Billy, clever as he knew himself to be, once, as other clever people had done before, made a mistake. His mistake was supposing that there

were no revenue boats near, when there were two, well
armed, close at hand; and he was caught napping in
consequence on board a lugger, with a full cargo of
tubs in her.

His day was come—there was no help for it—he was
a prisoner, but, like a man, he was not cast down,
not he; he laughed and joked, and sang as stoutly as
ever. He was taken on board a man-of-war, and
offered his choice—to go to gaol for a year with hard
labour, or to serve his Majesty for the same period.
Billy was a sailor, every inch of him.

"Serve his Majesty—of course I will—God bless
him," he exclaimed, and he thus became a man-of-war's
man. But now arrived the most cruel cut of all.

"I admire your spirit, my man," said the officer.
"You promise to serve his Majesty, and you shall forthwith do so. As a reward for your willingness, you are
appointed first mate of his Majesty's cutter, *Scourge*,
employed in the revenue service. Here is your
warrant."

"I would rather go to prison," said Billy.

"You have promised to serve his Majesty," answered
the officer.

"Oh, if that was understood," cried Billy, "so I
will. Look out for squalls, my hearties," he exclaimed,
turning round to where he saw several of his friends
standing who had come to attend his trial. "I have
promised to serve his Majesty, and I intend to do my
duty. You knows me. Remember, too, I knows you,

and all your dodges, but don't expect any favour from me—so I says, look out for squalls."

Having delivered himself of this harangue, Billy went on shore to make some necessary arrangements, and soon afterwards trod the deck of the *Scourge* as an officer. He was as good as his word. The cutter went to sea that afternoon, and the very next night made a rich capture of tubs of spirits and bales of silks. She soon became noted for being the most successful cruiser on the station, and at the end of the year had made more captures than she had done during all her previous career. So delighted was the commander of the *Scourge* with his success, owing to the large amount of prize-money he received, that he did his utmost to persuade Combe to remain with him; but to this none of his arguments could induce his first mate to consent.

"I promised to serve King George for a year, and to assist in collecting his revenue for him," said Billy. "I have done so faithfully, as you know. I am now free to go where I will."

The following day the *Scourge* put into Portsmouth harbour. Billy took his traps, went on shore, claimed his discharge, received it and his prize-money, and forthwith started for his native place, Hamble, a village on a stream of the same name, close to the mouth of the Southampton Water.

He was cordially welcomed on his arrival by his old friends, particularly by the fairer portion of them, among whom he was a great favourite, but more espe-

cially by Mary Dawson, the prettiest girl in the village.
Billy found himself in clover, for he had had much
hard work in the cutter, constantly at sea, and seldom
on shore, and he now the more felt inclined to enjoy
himself to the utmost.

Mary sat by his side and filled his pipe when it was
out, and replenished his glass when it was empty. He
warbled forth his best songs with a joyous voice, and
afterwards danced his best hornpipe with Mary, bounding about and shrieking with glee. He vowed that
though it might be a very fine thing to be a king's
officer, and wear a uniform, for his part he was heartily
glad to be free of it, and would be at the old work as
soon as he could. He wound up his exploits of the
evening by vowing to Mary, that after he had made a
few successful trips, he would come back and marry
her if she would have him, which, with many a blush,
she promised.

Some days after the evening when Billy made his
vows to Mary Dawson, a large craft might have been
seen steering through the Needles passage between the
Isle of Wight and the main, with a fresh breeze from
the north-east. She was a remarkably fine vessel, of
great beam and power, and carried four long guns of
heavy metal upon her decks, so that whatever work her
crew might have in hand, they would be able to fight
about it, if any one attempted to impede them. She
might have measured eighty tons, or rather more,
perhaps, I am not sure, but certainly not less, and

carried an enormous spread of canvas, new and white as the driven snow. Some twenty stout fellows walked her decks, with a strong spice of reckless daring in their countenances, and a costume which had no pretensions to uniformity, though affecting a considerable degree of nautical dandyism. Though the craft was built for speed and fitted for fighting, she certainly did not look like a king's ship, nor were her crew like man-o'-war's men. What she was her deeds will hereafter show.

On one side lay the coast of Hampshire, with its richly-cultivated fields, its ancient forest renowned in history, and its numerous country mansions; on the other the lofty cliffs and sunny downs of the beautiful Isle of Wight. The long outstretching beach of Hurst, with its sturdy round castle, was on her weather-quarter, and broad on her beam lay the Shingles, their small, yellow head just showing above water, and the wide expanse of foaming broken waves which surrounded them warning the mariner against a too near approach. On her weather or starboard-bow might be seen in the distance the high sandy cliffs of Hardle, and almost ahead the more elevated headland of Christchurch, with its town and the spire of its cathedral a little way inland. The vessel clove her way rapidly through the water. The dancing waves sparkled brightly in the rays of the rising sun, which threw a ruddy glow over the topmost pinnacles of the Needle rocks then close on her lee-bow. In those days they consisted of three lofty chalk rocks, two of them joined together at their

summits, but time, which spares so little, has spared
not them, and the fragment which connected them has
long since been precipitated into the depths below,
though they still proudly rear their heads, towering
above the fierce billows which rage during the storms of
winter at their base. The ship had just passed them,
and had opened Scratchall's Bay to the south-west of
them, when she might be said to be fairly in the British
Channel.

  " Now I feel myself once more a man," exclaimed,
in a joyous tone, a fine active-looking fellow, who had
been for some time walking the deck in silence, now gazing aloft with a satisfied eye at the trim of the sails, now
casting a glance over the side, or watching the passing
cliffs to see how fast the vessel slipped through the water.
" Isn't she a darling, Jim ?" he continued, turning to a
man who stood near him; " what a clean run she has,
and her bows—don't they just cut like a knife ? Look
at her canvas, what a spread of it she has—why,
there's enough there to carry you to heaven, Jim. I
should like to have a spanking breeze to try her, and
then if she just don't go along to astonish them, my
name isn't Billy Combe."

  The speaker was in truth the famed Billy Combe and
no other; now master and part owner of the *Rapid*,
just launched, and as fast a craft as ever sailed from
Hamble Creek. I have not yet described Billy. His
good looks did not consist so much in his height or
size, as in his active figure, his florid complexion, his

clear, open blue eye, his light curling locks, and his well-formed mouth and white teeth. Jim Dore was his first mate, and, if unlike him in some respects, he resembled him strongly in his attachment to smuggling.

"Keep her up a little bit, Tom," said the captain, turning to the man at the helm. "Here, my boys, take a pull of the main-sheet, and she'll lay well into Christchurch Bay; an inch or two of the jib-sheet now—there, that will do."

The vessel, hauled closer on a wind, heeled slightly over, and darted like an arrow with her head towards the shore.

"I'll tell ye what I'll do, Jim," observed the captain, as he walked the deck with his mate, every step showing the elasticity of his spirits, "we'll just heave her to while I go on shore for an hour or so, see Tom Doxton and the other spotsmen, arrange about collecting the people, and settle the time for running the crop, look in at the Haven House, get a swig of Betsy Sellers' ale, and then away for Cherbourg—eh, Jim? I should like to see the pretty craft with a full cargo in her; why, she'll be as stiff as a house. Bless her, she is a beauty!"

And with an eye of pride Billy surveyed over and over again every portion of his newly-purchased vessel —partly purchased, by-the-bye, with the prize-money he had gained while doing duty in the revenue service.

The town of Christchurch is situated on a shallow

arm of the sea, or lagoon, about three miles from the
coast, and at the entrance of this lagoon, on the west
side, is a sandy spot on which still stands a public-
house called the Haven House, then kept by a buxom
widow, a Mrs. Sellers, and the resort of seafaring men,
boatmen, and fishermen, but more especially of
smugglers. To the east, along the coast, Hardle Cliff
extends towards Lymington, with the small villages of
Ashe and Barton on its summit, and to the west and
south rises the high rugged promontory called Christchurch Head, while the coast, then trending to the
south, is indented with the bays of Poole, Studland,
and Swanwich. In less than an hour the *Rapid* lay
with her fore-sheet to windward, hove-to in Christchurch Bay, while Combe went on shore. After calling
at several cottages, and speaking to several people,
Billy took his way to the Haven House, a dark red-
brick building, with narrow gable ends, and outhouses
of lower proportions behind it. On one side was the
bar-room and kitchen all in one; on the other, a little
parlour with sanded floor, for the accommodation of
those who wished for privacy. Billy Combe entered the
bar-room with the independent air of a man who knows
that he is welcome, and the first person he encountered
was the landlady, the buxom widow Sellers. She
uttered a faint scream of surprise as she beheld him.
and a ruddy hue overspread her well-filled neck and
cheeks.

"Ah, Mr. Combe, is that you, indeed?" she exclaimed. "I thought you had forgotten me now you have turned king's officer."

"Forgotten you, Betsy! not I, forsooth. But, widow," continued Billy, seating himself on a bench at no great distance, it must be owned, from the landlady, "I'm no longer a king's officer, but am about the old work again, and, by-the-bye, Betsy, what do you think? I'm going to be spliced at last—hard and fast."

"Spliced!" ejaculated the widow, gasping for breath, "to whom?"

"Ah, that I shan't say, just to tease you," answered Billy, laughing; "a pretty girl, you may be sure."

"A mere girl! and is she better than a ——. Has all you said come to this—after what you have done— oh, Billy, Billy, how could you?" and the widow burst into tears.

Billy Combe was astonished, confounded. What had he done to make the widow weep? He did all he could to dry her tears, and to soothe her spirits, but in vain. She ended by being in a violent rage with him, and might have proceeded to extremities had not the arrival of some other persons put an end to this inter-view. With one of the strangers Billy retired into the parlour, to hold a conference of some importance, while the widow dried her tears, and put on a smiling coun-tenance to receive her guests, but she nevertheless treasured up her feelings in her heart, and vowed deadly vengeance against the betrayer of her happiness.

The rollicking captain of the *Rapid* having finally concluded all his arrangements in the private parlour of the Haven House, swallowed a tankard of the hostess's best ale, and giving her a parting salute, which she took with a bad grace, hurried down to his boat, and was quickly on board. The sails were immediately filled on the larboard tack, and with a flowing sheet the vessel ran across channel towards Cherbourg.

"Billy Combe, Billy Combe, you had better not have meddled with the widow," observed Jim Dore, with a laughing countenance, when his captain told him the story of the landlady's love. "Them widows is ticklish creatures, depend on it."

I have not time to describe how Billy Combe met a number of friends at Cherbourg, how he purchased a valuable cargo of brandy and silks, and how without loss of time he again got under weigh for the English coast. Scarcely had the *Rapid* put to sea than it came on to blow very hard from the north-east, with frequent squalls of rain and hail, so that Billy had as good an opportunity as his heart could desire of trying the weatherly qualities of his new craft.

"She behaves like a duck, that she does, the beauty!" he exclaimed, wiping the salt spray from his eyes with the back of his rough hand. "Wouldn't she go along just, if we had to run for it from a king's cruiser! I wouldn't give her up as long as I'd a stick standing or a keel to run on. that I know."

As night approached the wind increased, blowing dead on end from the Needles, but Combe still cracked on sail in the cutter; for he was not the man to miss being up to his time, and not having expected a foul wind he had spent a longer period at Cherbourg than he ought to have done. During the first part of the night they had an increasing moon, which, as the rapidly passing clouds ever and anon left it unobscured, afforded them just sufficient light to see the huge waves which came tumbling towards them, and enabled them to luff up in time to avoid their breaking on board, as also to steer clear of any vessel which might be standing across their course. When, however, towards the morning, the moon sunk beneath the horizon, and the clouds thickened in the sky, the darkness became so intense that they could scarcely see the noses on each other's faces, much less a fathom beyond the bowsprit. The captain now thought it better to shorten sail, so they got the storm-jib on her, and set the trysail, when away she went as merrily again as before.

" If this weather holds all to-morrow night, we are in high luck," observed Billy, " for the revenue cruisers will never think of coming out to look for us, and we shall have plenty of time to run all our cargo comfortably, except the red-coats on the shore take it into their heads to trouble us ; but if Doxton manages properly they will all be off at Keyhaven while we are getting the things on shore."

While he was speaking a sudden squall, stronger than before had blown, laid the vessel completely on her beam ends. Combe ran to the helm, for the man who was steering was thrown with violence on the deck, and seizing the tiller put up the helm.

"Lower away with the trysail—up with the jib," he sung out. Before much damage was done the vessel righted, and ran off before the wind.

The jib was then hauled down, and the trysail being again set, a lull was watched for, and the vessel brought gradually up with her head to the wind, and her fore-sheet to windward. There she lay, bobbing away like a duck upon the waves, but without taking a drop of water over her decks. Thus passed the night, during which the captain, who was naturally rather anxious, was, like a good seaman, constantly on deck.

The morning was approaching, but the thick, misty

atmosphere retarded the appearance of day; when just as he began to see rather more than an inch or so beyond his nose, as he was casting a glance of his weather eye to windward, he fancied he discerned through the darkness a towering mass bearing down towards him. At that moment the clouds breaking away in the east, a gleam of pale light was shed over the face of the deep. He looked again, the dark mass he had seen was the hull and sails of a ship running down channel.

" A sail close on the weather-bow," cried the look-out forward.

" Hard up with the helm," sung out Billy, " let draw the fore-sheet—keep her away, or the ship will be into us."

The vessel's sails were filled, and away she darted through the foaming waves, her main boom almost grazing the sides of a sloop of war, which came rolling down past her before the gale.

" What craft is that?" cried a voice through a speaking-trumpet from the deck of the ship.

" The Bow-wow-wow," responded Billy.

" What do you say?" cried the same voice.

" The ha! ha! ha!" replied Billy, and the ship was out of hearing. " I knows her," he observed, with a nod of the head; " she's the *Orestes* brig, and a fast craft she is, with a man who knows how to handle her as skipper. We must not show that we have reason to shun her though."

Billy kept his eye upon her movements. His answers did not appear to have been satisfactory, for presently she was seen to bring her broadside to the wind, the after yards were braced sharp up on the larboard tack, the head yards followed, and she stood away on a bowline, ready to tack back towards the *Rapid*.

"Is that your dodge, my lad?" said Billy, on the first indications of what she was about. "Lower away the trysail, my boys; set the mainsail; two reefs in it will do; out with the second jib. Bear a hand, my hearties; that ship is sent to look after us, so we've no time to lose. We shouldn't find her company pleasant, I can tell you."

The men scarcely needed any advice to stimulate them to exertion, for they one and all at once comprehended the dangerous position in which they were placed.

The vessel's best point of sailing was close hauled on a wind, and this Combe well knew was the *Orestes's* worst, though going free or before the wind she was a remarkably fast ship. His aim, therefore, since she had fortunately run past him, was to keep to windward of her, and as from her square rig she took a long time going about, to induce her to make as many tacks as possible, and thus to gain another advantage of her. The *Orestes* was now standing a little to the southward of east, close hauled on the larboard tack, while the *Rapid* was lying well up to the northward, on the other tack. As soon as the king's ship had hauled to the

H

wind she let fly one of her after guns as a signal for
Billy to heave-to.

"Talk away, old girl," said Billy, laughing; "you
may shout loud enough before I heed you."

Seeing that the *Rapid* held on her course regardless
of the signal, the *Orestes* fired shot after shot, the balls
flying wide of their mark, for with the heavy sea
running there was much difficulty in taking aim, and
naval gunnery was not in those days brought to the
perfection it is at present. Combe was aware that the
captain of the *Orestes* well knew that the *Rapid* would
not attempt to run before the wind, as his square-rigged
ship would then have the decided advantage of her,
and that he therefore hoped to capture her by jamming
her in with the land if he could not succeed in wing-
ing her with his shot. The *Rapid* consequently steadily
kept on her course to the northward, quickly increasing
her distance from the king's ship.

"She will be about soon, or she will be afraid of
missing us," observed Combe, "and then, my lads, it's
our turn. Ready about when you see her tack."

Scarcely had he spoken when the *Orestes* came slowly
up to the wind, her main yards were braced round, the
head sails followed, and away she dashed after her
chase.

"Now, my lads, look out for a lull," cried the captain of the *Rapid*. "Let fly the jib sheet, down with
the helm, Jim. That's it, beautifully. Let draw the
foresail. Oh, she's a darling!"

And the *Rapid* coming round in a third of the time the king's ship had taken, bounded away over the foaming waves with her head to the eastward, the sea breaking over her bows, and deluging her decks fore and aft; but her hatches were securely battened down, and not a drop got below. The people in the *Orestes*, enraged at the obstinacy and daring of the smuggler's crew,

redoubled their efforts to hit her, some of their shot passing very close, but none had yet come on board. At last one passed right through her mainsail.

"If it comes to that," exclaimed Combe, with an expression of anger his countenance seldom wore, " I'll show you that two can play at that game."   On this

he beckoned his crew aft. "Now, my lads, I've just this
to say to you," he began. "All I'm worth in the world
floats in this craft. It's hanging work to fire into a
king's ship, you know; but, for my part, I'd sooner
sink than be taken or lose my vessel. Will you stand
by me?"

"Never fear, Combe, we'll stand by you to a man,"
cried Jim Dore and the rest of the crew. "We are
ready to fight if you like it."

"Well then, my fine lads, let's train our lee guns aft,
and try to knock some of the feathers out of yon fine bird."

No sooner proposed than done. The two starboard
guns were loaded, and run out at the ports, and as the
Orestes offered a better mark for their aim than they
had done for hers, several of their shot took effect.
Combe watched them with an anxious eye, for it was
a hazardous game he was playing.

"I'll just take a shot and see what I can do," he
said, and watching till he brought his gun well on
with her foremast, he fired. The sea at that moment
lifted the stern of the cutter, and the shot flew higher
than he intended, though not than he wished, for it
knocked away the fore-topmast staysail sheet close at
the clew of the sail, which, fluttering wildly in the
gale, was almost torn to shreds before it could be hauled
down, while the ship, deprived of her head sail, flew
up into the wind. "Ha! ha!" exclaimed Combe,
clapping his hands with glee, "another shot like that
and we shall soon part company."

It was some time before a new sail could be bent,
and the delay enabled the *Rapid* to work considerably
ahead of her pursuer, but her position was still very
critical. A shot might carry away her mast or spars,
the wind might shift and throw her into the jaws of
the enemy, or it might drop altogether, and then the
boats would capture her to a certainty. The smugglers,
however, had now made their choice, and fighting was
to be the order of the day. In those good old times
they never thought of throwing the cargo overboard
or abandoning it to the enemy, and, in the present in-
stance, had they wished it, they could not have done
so without being seen. In consequence of the damage
she had received the *Orestes* was obliged to keep a
little off the wind, to run no risk of getting into it,
and being compelled to box off again, by which she
would have lost still more way; but as the *Rapid* crossed
her on the opposite tack, she revenged herself by letting
fly her whole broadside at her. The shot fell thick
round the vessel. One ball was more fatally directed
than the rest. It struck one of the smuggler's crew,
carrying away his arm, and dreadfully lacerating his
breast. A cry of agony escaped him as he fell bleed-
ing on the deck. His comrades attempted to raise him
and carry him below, but he entreated to be left on deck.

"It's all up with me," he ejaculated, faintly; "but
I'd like to see what happens. Here, Joe, just pass a
handkerchief round my shoulder, and then let me be;
there's no use doing more."

The smugglers brought up a mattress from below and placed their dying shipmate on it against the companion hatch, so that he could have a view of the enemy, as he desired. No one else was hurt, and the shot passing through the weather bulwarks, did no further damage.

As soon as the *Orestes* had hoisted a new fore-top-mast staysail, she tacked, on which the smuggler did the same, compelling the former soon afterwards to follow her example. This, however, was not the tack on which Combe wished to be, but he knew that the oftener he went about the oftener the brig of war would be obliged to do the same, as by standing on long on opposite tacks they would soon lose sight of each other, which with the thick weather there was would be quickly done. Thus they continued ploughing their way through the deep green froth-combed waves, tack and tack for some time, the smaller vessel evidently distancing her pursuer.

"We've got out of range of her guns, captain, at all events," said Jim Dore. "That was an unlucky shot for poor Jack Martin.—Well, Jack, how do you get on, my man?"

But the wounded seaman returned no answer. Dore went up to him; his eyes were glazed and staring. He knelt down by his side and took his hand; it was cold and clammy, and fell powerless on the deck. The poor fellow was dead. His last gaze had been one of defiance on those his lawless following had made his foes. His shipmates laying his body at the foot of the mast, covered it up with a sail till they had time to give it a sailor's simple burial. The sun was now high up in the heavens, though vainly attempting to break through the thick masses of dark clouds which floated rapidly past it, heavy showers of hail and rain every now and then continued falling, while the spray like a sheet covered the foaming waves.

The *Rapid*, like a sea-bird, stemmed buoyantly over it, dipping her bows now and then, as it were in sport, into the white-crested billows, and heeling over till her lee bulwarks were almost under water; while the heavier ship seemed, compared to her, to be labouring onwards through the stormy sea with pain and difficulty. Hour after hour passed thus away, and the day was drawing to a close, but still the king's cruiser continued the chase. At last, as the thick mist cleared away to windward for an instant the high chalk cliffs of the west end of the Isle of Wight appeared in sight.

"Huzza! my boys," exclaimed the captain, as the view welcomed his eyes, "let us once get well in with the land, and then good-bye to the Orestes. We shall get the young flood making up close in shore round the island, with smooth water, while she still has a tumbling sea, and an hour more of the ebb."

The smuggler now made a long reach, standing on till she was close under the cliffs of a beautiful part of the coast, some way to the eastward of Freshwater Bay, where she was in comparatively smooth water. She held her course till she looked as if she were about to rush upon the sandy beach, when her helm was put down, and away she went upon the other tack.

"There's less wind in here," observed Combe, whose complacency had considerably returned; "let's shake another reef out of the mainsail, and see if we can't jog her on a little faster. We must be off Christchurch to-night, somehow. Luff her up a bit, Joe; see how she shoots ahead; so—steady—that will do."

The smugglers, who had for some time past been standing with their hands in their pea-coat pockets, without employment, were now all upon the alert. The reef was shaken out and the sail hoisted up in a moment. It was now tack and tack every instant, the *Rapid* standing on till she seemed almost upon the rocks; but Combe knew every inch of the coast, and took advantage of every little bay and each channel between the rocks to make good his way out of the strength of the ebb. Often it appeared impossible that his vessel could escape from the dark rocks above water, and the hidden rocks covered with foaming breakers by which she was surrounded, but with wonderful sagacity Combe steered her amid the dangers, and was soon again in the open sea. By the time the rays of the setting sun, which for an instant burst forth from amid the dark clouds, cast a ruddy glow upon the white summits of the Culver cliffs at the east end of the island, the sloop of war, as seen from the *Rapid's* decks, was hull down to leeward. Again the opaque clouds closed in, the thick mist came down over the land and sea, and darkness rapidly approached. Less and less distinct appeared the lofty sails of the king's cruiser, till at last the sharpest eye on board could no longer discern them.

"Huzza! my lads, we've shown a clean pair of heels this time, and now we must see about getting the things on shore. I promised to be off Christchurch Head by twelve to-night. It's a long way from this, but it must be done. We'll see if the *Rapid* can't go as fast through the water before the wind as she has done close hauled. What say you, Jim,—shall we run through the Needles, or round by the back of the island again?"

"I should say through the Needles," answered the mate. "We shall have smooth water and the best part of the ebb, and there's no cruiser will ever think of looking out for us in this weather."

The *Rapid* was accordingly kept close hauled, and after numerous tacks she weathered St. Helens, and easing off her mainsheet, stood away with a flowing sail through the passage between the island and Spithead. Dark as it was the smugglers' keen eyes, sharpened by long practice, could sufficiently discern the shores on either side of the Solent to enable them to hold their course down the centre of the channel. Having made Cowes Point, the remaining reefs were shaken out of the mainsail, the squaresail was set, and keeping before the wind, the vessel was steering directly for the Needles passage, where I first introduced her to my readers.

How changed now was the scene from what it was on that morning. Then it was a view of calm beauty and sunshine, now all was darkness and tempest. The wind whistled loudly, the wild waves foamed and fretted, the lightning flashed, but the smugglers' hearts were undaunted. The lights on Hurst beach enabled them to steer clear through the dangerous passage, their ears deafened with the loud roar of the surges as they dashed furiously against the Needle rocks, but they threaded their way in safety and were once more in the open sea. It wanted still an hour to midnight. Taking in her squaresail and two reefs in the mainsail, for it was still blowing almost as hard as ever, the cutter hauled up a little for Christchurch Bay. At last the dark outline of Christchurch Head appeared on the larboard bow, the *Rapid* was rounded to, and a lantern hoisted three times to the mast-head. To those not watching for it, it might have appeared like some meteor or a deception of the sight. The signal was speedily answered from the shore, to the no small satisfaction of the smugglers. The goods were now quickly got up on deck ready for landing. A quarter of an hour had passed when several boats were seen pulling towards them. A light was shown from the headmost one, and a pistol flashed directly after it.

"Boat ahoy!" hailed the captain of the *Rapid;* "who are you looking for?"

"A friend, a pipe, and a glass of grog," answered a voice from the boat.

"All right; come on board," responded Combe.

On this the boats pulled alongside, when a few words served to explain the occurrences of the day, though little time was expended in conversation.

The crew of the smuggler now set to work to load the boats, which, however, being of small size, for the sake of running into shallow water, could venture, with the heavy sea there was running, only to carry a small portion of the goods at a time. They had already made several trips, when from information Combe received from the shore, he determined to land himself in order to superintend the transportation of the goods further inland. Leaving, therefore, the *Rapid* in charge of Jim Dore, with directions, should an enemy appear, to stand out to sea and to try the swiftness of his heels, he leaped into one of the laden boats and steered for the beach. The wind had by this time considerably abated, the rain ceased, the clouds cleared away, and the moon shed a bright light upon the waters. This was what those engaged in their lawless occupation would particularly have avoided. The darker the night and the worse the weather the better they were pleased. Combe, however, ascertained, much to his satisfaction, that the dragoons stationed in the neighbourhood had gone off towards Milford, so there was little chance of interruption from them, and for other enemies he cared little.

The spot where the run was made was a narrow, shingly beach, at the foot of the long range of high cliffs I have already described as extending between Christchurch and Lymington. As Combe stepped on shore, he found a number of people collected; some were employed in unloading the boats, while others were carrying the things up the cliffs, where carts were ready to convey them to the depôts far inland. The greater portion was still piled up upon the beach, above high-water mark, for so steep and difficult was the path up the cliff that one man could convey only a single tub or a small case of silks at a time. They appeared like ants as they wound their way in a long line along the narrow path up the cliff, where, having deposited their loads, they returned by an almost perpendicular descent to the beach.

There might have been sixty persons, or more, engaged in the work, besides the crew of the Rapid, every one of them armed to the teeth with pistols, blunderbusses, and swords, or pikes. Some were in the dress of countrymen, with smock-frocks or velveteen jackets, others were evidently seamen, and some few who appeared to be directing the rest, were, by the tones of their voices, belonging to a higher station in society. The presence of Combe among them reanimated them all to greater exertions, for already a valuable portion of the night had been spent, and much remained to be done. At last it was found impossible to convey all the goods away into the interior of the

country before daybreak, when Combe, consulting with
the man called Doxton and others of his chief assistants,
it was determined to stow them away in the vault
often used for that purpose, beneath some ruins situated
on the side of a ravine which ran up from the shore a
short distance to the eastward.   The party accordingly
divided : Doxton with one gang of armed men mounted
the cliffs to escort the carts to a place of safety, while
Combe remained to superintend the removal of the
rest of the goods into the vault.   The ruin had in the
olden days of Rome's supremacy been a chapel dedicated to the Holy Virgin, the protector of mariners, and
has long since totally disappeared, although the vault
probably still remains covered up by rubbish and over-
grown by green herbage.   Combe had about ten of his
own crew with him and twenty landsmen, so that in
a couple of trips the whole of the goods on shore were
conveyed out of sight, and, as he judged, the hold of
the *Rapid* was almost cleared, when, as he was standing in front of the ruins telling off the people as they
came in, he was startled by several flashes to seaward
and the report of fire-arms.   He rushed to the edge of
the cliff, whence, through his night-glass, he could better
observe what was going forward.   The moon sinking
low towards the horizon cast her light upon the white
sails of a tall ship in the offing, while the *Rapid*, with
every stitch of canvas she could carry, was standing
away to the westward, returning the fire, from what
he judged from the flashes of the guns to be one or

more boats chasing her, though the darkness prevented
their movements being clearly seen.

Combe watched the scene with intense interest, his
hands almost crushing the spy-glass he held in his
grasp.

"I would give a thousand pounds to be on board
now," he exclaimed to himself; "but Dore is a man,
and will fight the vessel to the last. If he can get
round St. Alban's Head by the time the moon goes
down, it's hard if he don't manage to weather on the
revenue cruiser, whoever she may be, in the dark, and
be off to the coast of France. Bravo, Jim! fire away,
my lad! Ah, the *Rapid* shows her heels, and the boats
may catch her if they can. Now she has only got the
big one to deal with, and with this leading wind, if she
keeps well in shore, where the other can't follow, she's
safe."

While he was speaking, the flashes from the guns appeared to be growing further and further apart, and it
was evident that the revenue boats had been discovered
by the smuggler before they were alongside, in time for
them to fill her sails and stand away from them, and
Combe judged rightly that Dore had fired at them
merely to draw them on and attract their attention
from the shore.

Combe was soon joined by some of the smugglers,
who had likewise been startled by the firing, while
others came hurrying up from the beach with the same
intelligence. A large band were thus soon collected,

endeavouring to discern through the darkness the manœuvres of the vessels, making their observations with violent oaths and exclamations, and vowing vengeance against those who dared to interfere with their proceedings.   While thus occupied, they were suddenly aroused by loud shouts, cries, and execrations, the report of pistols, and the tramping of feet.   Combe, followed by the rest of the men, rushed down the cliff, where they were met by several of their people, laden with goods, and pursued by a strong party of seamen, led on by an officer in naval uniform.   The two parties met at the entrance of the ravine, and so impetuous was the charge of the king's seamen, that the smugglers were driven back several paces before they were able to make a stand; pistol-shots were rapidly exchanged, their flashes lighting up the scene, the clash of cutlasses mingling with the shouts and fierce execrations of the combatants.   Combe, rallying his people, who were soon joined by the remainder of their friends, again led them on, when he encountered the royal officer at the head of his men.

"Yield, you rascal, yield," cried the officer, aiming a blow with his cutlass at Combe's head, "some of your fellows have given us trouble enough to-night, and you shall pay for it."

"I never give in while I can fight," returned the smuggler, as he parried the blow and drew a pistol from his belt.

His anger was up, for he guessed by these words

that it was one of the officers of the *Orestes* opposed to him. He fired—the officer, with a groan, staggered and fell, and the smugglers at the same time making a desperate rush, drove back the seamen, disheartened by the loss of their leader, to the beach. Another officer in vain endeavoured to urge them on; the smugglers, grown desperate, were too many for them. The king's seamen fought well and kept their enemies at bay, but at last were driven back and compelled to save their lives in the boats. This was all Combe required to enable his friends to carry off the remainder of the goods, and as soon as this was accomplished he sounded a retreat, on which the smugglers instantly dispersed with such rapidity up the cliffs that by the time the man-of-war's men again landed not one of them was to be seen.

The next morning the dead body of the officer, who proved to be the master of the *Orestes*, was found, but none of the crew could swear to the person who fired the shot which killed him, nor were any hopes entertained by the authorities of discovering the guilty man. The commander of the *Orestes*, it appeared, had from the first received information of the run intended to be made near Christchurch, and was on the look-out for the smuggler when the gale I have described came on; and on losing sight of her at the east end of the island, after beating some hours more to windward in the vain hope of falling in with her, he put the ship about and stood back for Christchurch Bay.   He

arrived, as we have seen, just in time to be too late.
The master, with two boats, was accordingly despatched
to surprise the *Rapid*, but Jim Dore was too wide awake
to be taken at advantage. The result of the attempt
has already been shown.

We must now change the scene to the private parlour
of the Haven House, on the evening after the run.
Before a table, on which stood sundry bottles, jugs
glasses, and meerschaums, with tobacco-boxes and other
apparatus for smoking, sat three men, with one of
whom the reader is well acquainted, being no other than
the redoubted Billy Combe; another was a man of
whom I have spoken, Doxton by name; and the third
was a person of greater pretensions, though of his re-
spectability others may think differently, as he was a
partner of the London house on whose account the
silks and laces had been bought. Business had been
got over and their glasses replenished.

"This is a bad affair, the death of the master of the
Orestes," observed the respectable merchant; "it will
make the revenue officers more on the alert."

"It couldn't be helped," answered Combe in a careless tone. "If I had not shot him, he would have
shot me or some better man."

"What, it was you who shot him!" said the merchant. "I thought you had more discretion."

"I did shoot him, and I scorn to deny it," answered
Combe, boldly; "I was defending my right, and would
do the same again to any one who interfered with me."

I

"But you may get yourself into trouble if you run such risks, and then whom shall we employ to bring over our silks?" argued the merchant.

"My advice, Combe, to you, is, that you should get quietly over to the coast of France till all inquiries about the death of the officer are at rest," observed

Doxton. "It will be known to a certainty that you were the leader of the party, and you will be made answerable."

"Do, my good friend, do take care of yourself; we cannot afford to lose you," added the merchant.

While this discussion was going forward, Mrs. Sellers knocked at the door, and being told to enter, placed in Billy's hand a note, which ran thus:

"DEAR CAPTAIN,

"I write this, which a French lugger will carry over to you, from Cherbourg. We had a sharp run, but doubled on the big one, and stole away to windward of her, while she thought she had run us on shore dead to leeward. We want you over here, and no one more so than

"Yours,

"JIM DORE."

"Huzza!" exclaimed Combe; "the *Rapid's* safe, and now I care for nothing. I say, Betsy, just bring in some paper and ink, not forgetting a pen. I want to write a letter home, just to tell them I shall not be back for some time, and then I'm off for France."

He accordingly set to work, and wrote several letters, rather laconic they certainly were, which he committed to the care of Mrs. Sellers. On the superscription of one of them was Mary Dawson's name. When the widow saw it, her eye kindled and her lips curled with anger, and poor Mary never received his letter.

When Combe received his note, the lugger was employed in running her cargo, and by daybreak she was again to sail. Combe had made his arrangements, and was walking down to the beach, where a boat was waiting to convey him on board the Frenchman, when he found himself on a sudden surrounded by a number of armed men, and before he had time to make any resistance, his hands were bound behind him, he was lifted on horseback, and carried off far inland, escorted by a party of dragoons.

Combe was a bold fellow, and could look at things on their black side without trembling, but he at once saw the critical position in which he was placed. For two days the party travelled on, stopping only a sufficient time to rest their horses; when at length they reached London, and the smuggler found himself the inmate of a prison, without a soul to speak to or advise with. He had been a prisoner for some days, and even his buoyant spirits were at a low ebb, when, as he was seated in his cell, resting his head upon his hands, and giving way to melancholy reflections, the door opened, and a person entered. He looked up, and beheld, by the dim light of the lamp, the girl he loved, his own Mary Dawson. Springing on his feet, he clasped her in his arms. She sobbed on his bosom; and even his stout heart was moved almost to tears. She told him that it was reported that affairs would go hard with him on his trial, but that Jim Dore had come over from France, and had collected plenty of money to employ the best counsel for his defence. Combe, in return, endeavoured to cheer her spirits, and to assure her that all would go well.

"But you did not murder the officer?" said Mary: "surely you could not kill anybody?"

"Murder! no," answered Combe, proudly; "cowards only murder. But don't ask me, Mary—what is done I cannot now undo. Thank you, my own Mary, for all you have done for me; and tell Dore, if he can get leave to see me, to come without delay."

The gaoler now came in to tell Mary she must quit her lover.

The next day Dore arrived with a lawyer, and Combe's defence was drawn out with considerable ability, though, as the accuser was unknown, there was some difficulty in doing so. At last the trial came on: Combe was placed in the dock, and in the witness-box appeared a female—she turned her head towards the prisoner, and he beheld the vindictive features of Widow Sellers. Several of Combe's friends had come up to London to attend the trial. The business of the day commenced; the witnesses were examined. Mrs. Sellers swore that she had heard him acknowledge that he had killed the master of the *Orestes;* Doxton was brought forward, and compelled to confirm the statement; and then two of the seamen of the *Orestes* swore that they saw him fire the fatal shot; one of the smugglers being brought forward to prove that he was one of those engaged, and at the head of the party. Against this mass of evidence it was impossible to contend successfully. The jury returned a verdict of guilty, and the judge, putting on the black cap, pronounced his sentence. He was condemned to be hung, as a pirate, in chains, on the banks of the Thames.

Combe heard his doom, like a brave man, without trembling, though he afterwards entreated that Mary might be conveyed home without being told of his condemnation, observing—

"It would break my heart to see her in tears, poor girl, and could do her no good. But, Jim, if you could manage it, though I was not given much to church-going, I should like to rest quietly in our own church-yard, and then mayhap she would come sometimes and watch over me."

Dore, as he wrung his comrade's hand, promised to obey his wishes.

In those days, the bank of the Thames, near Black-wall, was adorned with a row of lofty gibbets, on which hung the ghastly remains of several pirates and murderers on the high seas, as a warning to all the passers-by to avoid a similar destiny.

I am not fond of describing horrors, and shall there-fore not detail the execution of my hero. The sun went down and rose again, and men and boys were hawking about the streets of London, "A full, true, and particular Account of the Life and Adventures, and the last dying Speech and Confession of the bold Smuggler, William Combe, who murdered the Master of his Majesty's sloop *Orestes*, and was executed this morning."

That night was one of storm and rain, and the bodies of the malefactors swayed to and fro in the gale, while the creaking of the gibbets and the clanking of the chains added their mournful music to the howling of the wind. Just after nightfall, while the tempest was at its height, two men approached the gibbet whereon hung the body of the smuggler, and, climbing to the top, set to work with files and chisels to free it from its chains. So well did they ply their instruments, that in a short time their work was accomplished, when, lowering the body to the ground, they bore it to a light cart waiting at hand. As soon as it was stowed within, and carefully covered up, they drove off at a rapid rate towards the south. Several times they changed horses, which were standing out in readiness for them, and long before the morning dawned, they stopped at the entrance of Hamble churchyard.

The incumbent of Hamble was a worthy good man, of even temper and peaceable disposition, seeking to live in charity with all men, though rather afraid of his lawless and unruly parishioners. He had long retired to rest, when he was aroused by a loud knocking at the door of the parsonage, and a voice summoning him to dress and come down with his prayer-book in hand. Half asleep, he did as he was desired, supposing some dying person required the consolations of religion; but no sooner did he open his door, than he found himself surrounded by several men, who gently led him forward.

" No harm is intended, sir," said one, in a respectful tone, "but we have no time to lose. All we wish you to do is to perform the funeral service over the body of a parishioner, and to ask no questions."

The good priest felt that he had no resource but to consent, and soon entering the churchyard, he found himself standing at the head of a newly-opened grave, at the other end of which he saw the old sexton, with the implements of his calling, while around stood a number of persons, chiefly in the rough dresses of seamen, a lantern here and there held by some of them, throwing a pale uncertain light over the ghastly scene. He had scarcely been there a minute, when wheels were heard rapidly approaching, and soon afterwards several men appeared, bearing in their arms a human body, wrapped up in a large sea-coat, which they placed carefully on the ground by the side of the newly-made grave, exposing the features to view. The people crowded round it, when a young woman who had been before standing aloof with two or three other females, rushed forward, and threw herself by the side of the corpse, exclaiming—

"Let me see him! let me see him!—they could not have been so barbarous as to murder him!"

But when the poor girl beheld the pallid and distorted features of her dead lover, uttering a loud shriek, she fell back fainting into the arms of her friends. It is extraordinary with what care and forethought the smugglers had made arrangements for fulfilling their friend's dying request. A coffin was brought forward, into which the body was placed, and the lid being fastened down, the curate was requested to read the funeral service, which he did in a solemn, serious tone.

in which a slight agitation might now and then have been perceptible. As the coffin was lowered into the grave, on the lid appeared, in brass letters, the name of "WILLIAM COMBE."

"There," exclaimed Jim Dore, with an unusual tremulousness in his voice, as the earth closed over the grave, "I've done my duty to the poor fellow, and a braver man, or a better messmate, than he who's gone to rest, I never hope to break biscuit with again."

Soon afterwards, a simple grave-stone was erected, on which was inscribed the name of "William Combe; Died A.D. 1789, Aged 30;" and every day, while flowers bloomed, was it encircled with a fresh wreath by the hand of love. Poor Mary remained faithful to her first affection, and even honest Jim Dore could not move her heart.

Mrs. Sellers was ever afterwards pointed at, as an example of the extremes to which a widow's vengeance might go when she is crossed in love. The smugglers deserted her inn, though it was still patronised by the revenue-men, but they only spent a quarter of what her former customers did; and she at length quitted the place, to avoid the sight of objects which recalled to her memory the loves she had so barbarously destroyed, though the Haven House remains to this day in much the same state as it then existed; and many a time is the tale told within its snug bar, by its seafaring occupants, of how the bold smuggler, Billy Combe,

was hung near Blackwall, on the Thames, for shooting
the master of the *Orestes*, and buried, the same
night, in Hamble churchyard, on the coast of Hampshire.

THE DESERTERS.

I.

In the summer of 1812, a fine ship was holding her course in solitary pride through the blue waters of the South Atlantic. Though her sides were lofty, and she carried a heavy battery of guns, with a numerous crew, neither had her canvas the cut, nor her yards the squareness, of those of a man-of-war. She was, in

truth, one of the richly-freighted barques belonging
to the powerful company of British merchants, under
whose fostering care our Indian empire had its rise and
progress till it became too vast for any but Imperial
rule. Every sail was set below and aloft, with studding-
sails on each side, to take advantage of the favourable
breeze which was sending her along at the rate of nine
knots an hour from the shores of England. Her course
was towards that surge-beaten rock which rears its lofty
summit, dark, rugged, and alone, from amid the ocean
depths—the island of St. Helena—a spot which was
afterwards to become famous throughout the world as
the prison and the tomb of the great Napoleon.

It is difficult clearly to describe the scene which the
Indiaman presented, with her crowded cabins supplied
with every article of luxury: the rich merchandise
below; the stores of provisions; the dark berths of the
seamen; the carpenters', blacksmiths', and tailors'
shops; the cow-house; the sheep-pens and hencoops;
the kitchen, with its ever active cook; the butcher and
baker following their avocations; people moving in all
directions; and the hum of voices heard from every
part;—these, with the dark line of guns lashed to her
bulwarks on each side, the snowy hammocks in the
nettings, the numerous boats, the clean decks, the ropes
fastened down, the tall masts, the outspreading yards,
the white sails, and the intricate tracery of the rigging,
forming a defined and familiar picture to a seaman's
eye; but to a landsman, who has never beheld the

like, appearing an almost incomprehensible mass of confusion.

The glowing sun of the tropics, now approaching the horizon, was casting his burning rays from an unclouded sky in a shower of golden refulgence upon the dark blue waters which rose and fell in gentle undulations, merely rippled over by the playful breeze, but unbroken save where they curled and leaped round the bows of the majestic ship as calmly she parted them asunder, or where her steady track was marked by a lengthened line of snowy whiteness. Her decks were crowded with people: the after-part with the officers and cabin passengers, while on the forecastle was collected the greater part of the crew; a few women—some natives of India, servants of the cabin passengers—and a considerable number of soldiers, mostly fresh recruits, for the service of the Company. The latter were raw youths, collected from all parts of the United Kingdom, of every sort of character and disposition, possessed of various degrees of education, and intended originally for different trades and professions, which many opposite motives had induced them to quit for the profession they had now adopted; and it was the duty of the older soldiers to amalgamate these very incongruous materials—a task not easy of accomplishment without the strictest discipline, firmness, and discretion, which latter quality was too often neglected, with the most fatal results, as the following narrative will show.

In those days it was the custom of the Company fre-

quently to disembark their newly-levied troops at St.
Helena, both to drill and discipline them, and to inure
them to a tropical climate, before they were exposed to
the hardships of actual warfare, as well as to make them
take their turn in garrisoning the island; a duty which
appears always to have been distasteful and irksome to
the young soldiers, from the unvaried routine, the constant parades, and rigid subordination to which they
were subjected, instead of beholding the wonders of the
East, which they had been taught to expect.

II.

Two young men were pacing together the short space
afforded them for a walk on the top-gallant forecastle—
a small deck raised above what is called the upper deck,
at the fore-part of a ship. They wore the military cap
and undress uniform of the other recruits, though the
manner in which they trod the deck showed that they
were accustomed to the sea, and there was that in their
air and appearance which distinguished them from the
rest of their comrades, and betokened them to be possessed of superior education. There appeared to be a
slight difference in their ages, and the eldest therefore
claims the first description. His figure was about the
middle height, strongly built, with well-knit limbs,
which gave promise of great bodily activity; his complexion was florid, with light closely-curling hair, while
his features were not only well-formed, but would have

been considered decidedly handsome and pleasing, had
not fierce and unrestrained passions already stamped
them with their indelible traces. His full grey eyes,
when his feelings were unexcited, looked so calm and
soft, that they appeared beaming with almost a woman's
tenderness, but on the slightest opposition to his will,
they instantly flashed with the angry blaze of his fiery
temper; and his mouth, that more certain index of
the disposition, betokened him to be a firm and fearless
character, more likely to attempt leading others, than
tamely to submit to dictation. The physiognomist
examining his countenance would at once have pronounced him to be possessed of qualities which, if
well-directed, might raise him to the most elevated
position, but which, were he left to his own devices,
would too probably prove the cause of his complete
destruction. Such was William Halliday.

He was the second son of a wealthy farmer in the
north of England, whose property bordered the sea-
coast. He had been sent to various schools, as well as
to one of the northern universities, but had, although
possessed of good abilities, been expelled from the latter
on account of his determined resistance to all authority.
At the same time that young Halliday was pronounced
an incorrigible reprobate by his masters, he was beloved
by his companions of the same age as himself for his
kind and generous disposition. He was at all times
the champion of those who were oppressed and unable
to defend themselves: often, too, would he bear the

punishment due to the faults of another boy, rather
than betray him to his superiors. He was always the
first to be accused when no other culprit could be found.
The behaviour of his masters by degrees hardened his
temper, and made him alike indifferent to punishment
or applause.   How little did his instructors imagine
the ruin they were working in a noble fabric! whereas
by judicious management from the first, his faults
would have been corrected, and his disposition unimpaired.   Notwithstanding his general idleness, he had
contrived to gain a considerable amount of information,
and his indulgent father had hopes of his reformation.
He listened calmly and leniently to his son's excuses
for his behaviour, forgave him, and told him that he
must henceforth make amends for his former wildness
by assisting him diligently in his business.   William
promised, and intended to perform his promise, but the
dull routine of a farmer's life was not at all to his taste ;
and though for a time he attended with tolerable regu-
larity to his duties, he gladly flew to other pursuits on
the slightest pretext.   Living close to the sea-shore, he
had from his boyhood been accustomed to pass much of
his time upon the ocean, and had become, by constant
practice, a bold and dexterous boatman. His delight
was to steer a light skiff he claimed as his own, at
early dawn, far out to sea, where, miles from land, he
would remain all day, revelling in the wild solitude
of the ocean, nor return till the sun warned him that
evening was approaching.   And often would he, in

mere sport, dart through the heaviest breakers, where few would venture to follow. By his courage and experience, indeed, the crew and passengers of a large ship wrecked on the coast were preserved—a gallant act, which gained him the applause and respect of all who heard of it, as well as the gratitude of those whose lives, at the risk of his own, he had preserved.

As yet, William Halliday, with all his errors, had been free from crime. His trials had not yet come. He was not to escape the fiery ordeal of temptation; and who, without firm principles—guardian angels, ever watchful by his side—can hope to escape unscathed? Unhappily he possessed not these; yet his thirst for excitement, and his love of enterprise, were the primary causes of his fall, rather than a vicious disposition. Had his father, instead of attempting to bring up one of his ardent temperament to the regular routine of his own calling, sent him at an early age to sea— where, while his dominant failings would have been corrected by strict discipline, his desire for change would have been fully satisfied before it had gained overpowering strength—he might have escaped the peculiar temptations to which he was subjected. But such was not to be. Let his example prove a warning to others; and let other fathers and masters remember his fate, when they discover similar dispositions in their sons or pupils.

His love of the excitement to be found on the ocean caused young Halliday to become acquainted with all

k

the seafaring men in the neighbourhood, some of whom were very bad characters. At that time the loose enforcement of the revenue laws gave encouragement to an extensive system of smuggling along all the coasts of England, and with many of the persons engaged in this illegal traffic he was consequently thrown in constant contact. Among the worst was a man of the name of Derrick, the owner of several smuggling craft. This man had long fixed his eye on young Halliday, calculating that he would be, from his intrepid character and social position, an able coadjutor in his plans. It was not long before he had an opportunity, of which he failed not to make use, of enticing the young man on board his cutter, and offering him a cruise to the coast of France. This offer was too willingly accepted, and frequently repeated; so that, although Halliday took no part in their business, he was completely committed with the smugglers, and very soon not only forgot the lawlessness of their proceedings, but by degrees, from assisting, he lent a hand in landing the goods from the vessel.

Young Halliday knew he was doing wrong, but he tried to persuade himself that, as he did not take any of the profits of these illegal transactions, he was not distinctly implicated. In this delusion, he continued to associate with the smugglers, and, as may be expected, was led from one thing to another, till he brought himself within the direct grasp of the law.

Early one morning his party, in landing a cargo of

goods, was attacked by the revenue officers; a scuffle ensued; blood was shed; several were wounded on both sides; and one man was cut down by Halliday, who forthwith fled from the fray—a murderer. Hurrying from the scene, he crossed the country on foot, met the mail going northward, and taking a seat on it, was carried to York. From this place he found his way to Hull, where he intended to ship as a seaman on board the first vessel about to sail; to what part of the world he cared not. As it happened, not one foreign-bound ship was likely to be ready for sea. He, however, found a vessel ready to sail for London, and in this he took his passage. The voyage lasted several days, during which young Halliday became acquainted with a person of indifferent character who introduced him to parties still worse in London. Once put on a wrong track, it is inconceivable how quick is the progress to destruction. Halliday could not be called deliberately bad; but his impulses and his heedlessness had been equally injurious. Ere he had entered life in the ordinary sense of the term, he was a ruined man. The consciousness of being a homicide, and that his character was altogether gone, impelled him to sink the deeper in guilt. He scarcely cared what came of him. In this state of mind, it is not to be wondered at that he took part in an enterprise which had for its object to rob a gentleman on his way home at night, and who was known to carry a considerable amount of valuable property on his person. This affair proved less advantageous than had been reckoned on.   The gentleman to be waylaid was well armed, and on being suddenly set upon, shot one of the robbers in the breast.   The others immediately fled.   The wounded man was taken into an adjoining cottage, which, strange to say, proved to be one inhabited by his wife, whom he had cruelly deserted; and the scene which ensued may be more easily imagined than described.

Now doubly guilty, Halliday felt that his life hung by a single hair.   Perhaps the wounded man, if lable to speak, would reveal his name and residence.   In this conjuncture he did what is probably done in many similar circumstances.   Having exchanged his apparel for a common working-dress, and otherwise disguised himself, he enlisted into the East India Company's service.   In those days few questions were asked about previous character, and a fine youth was not to be rejected.   He was at once admitted under a feigned name, and before many days elapsed, had joined the depôt of the Company's regiments, whence in a few weeks he embarked for India.

III.

Henry Hastings, the young man whom we have mentioned as being Halliday's companion on board the ship, had enlisted about the same time, but from different causes.   He had always been a favourite with the colonel of hussars and the officers quartered in the barracks of the little seaport town of which his father

was the rector. Of a much less robust frame than
Halliday, his figure would have conveyed the idea of
activity, and no small power of endurance. Mr.
Hastings, after taking a high degree at Oxford, became
a fellow of his college, where he continued to reside
for some years, till he accepted the living of Sand-

mouth, when it fell in. Naturally of retiring manners,
and possessing a poetical temperament, he had at no
time mixed in any but in the limited society of the
university, and with the world at large he was un-
acquainted. On his entering on the duties of his
profession he married an amiable young lady, who

died in a few years, after giving birth to two children —a son and a daughter. So completely were the thoughts of Mr. Hastings occupied with scientific and literary pursuits, and with what he considered the duties of his calling, that he appeared totally to forget the necessity of attending to his worldly affairs, and to the education of his children. Fortunately for them, on the death of his wife a widowed sister came to reside with him, and by her judicious management so corrected their failings, and excited their best qualities, that few more amiable or engaging children could be found. Julia Hastings grew up in time to be a lovely and charming girl, endued with good sense and talent, and a firmness of character which neither her father nor brother appeared to possess. Henry, though her senior by a year, unfortunately had not the settled principles, nor the determined spirit of his sister, though equalling her in amiability and a desire to do right, with even a more enthusiastic and romantic temperament. He had no vices, and many virtues, but they were all of a passive rather than of an active nature. Though books were his delight, his reading was too desultory and irregular to lead to any useful results; nor did any great improvement take place during the short time he was at the university. He had always admired the smart military carriage of the hussars, but the only amusement in which, like most men of his age, he indulged, was boating; and from his boyhood he had been accustomed to steer his light skiff over the dancing waven, and to manage her with considerable dexterity. It suited his romantic disposition. He loved to make excursions along the beautiful shores of his native county, to sail up its rivers, and visit its sheltered bays, till he almost fancied himself the explorer of new regions fertile and wealthy.

On Henry's return home after keeping his first college term, he brought with him to the vicarage a friend, whom he had known from his boyhood; and certainly Lionel Ravenhurst did full justice to his discrimination of character, for a more attractive person in mind, manner, and appearance could scarcely be met with. He came to enjoy a few days' yachting, which Henry had promised him, but his visit was prolonged for several weeks. Each day that the weather was favourable the friends spent upon the water, when Julia was their frequent companion; nor did her beauty and amiability fail to make a deep impression on the heart of their guest. At last he was compelled to leave them, to join his family abroad; and Julia only then began to discover how essential his presence was to her happiness.

Scarcely had young Ravenhurst gone, when Mr. Hastings was taken alarmingly ill, and before many days had passed, he died, bestowing a blessing on his children, and expressing a hope that they would be in some manner provided for. What a blow was this to Henry and his sister! Both were thrown suddenly on new resources, and with little hope of successfully overcoming the difficulties that presented themselves. One of the first things which Henry did was to examine

into the state of his father's affairs. To his consternation they were found in a very confused and embar-
rassed condition. His father had not consulted a rigor-
ous prudence in giving him an expensive university
education; and it would have been greatly more judicious, in the circumstances, had he placed his son in
some useful business. But regrets on these points
were now useless. All that could possibly be realised
for the family, including the aged aunt, was fifty
pounds a-year. Henry was overwhelmed with grief on
his sister's account. For himself he felt not; but to
leave one of so gentle a nature, and so gently nurtured,
to the indifference of the world—to compel her to seek
for subsistence in the capacity of a governess, to the
irritating annoyances of unmannered children—the
very thought was misery.

For some days his mind was in a state of anguish and
uncertainty. At last his resolution was taken. He
would devote all that remained of their father's property
to the support of his sister, and he would seek his
fortune in the world, and perhaps soon restore to her
the luxuries she had lost. She, with her aunt, might
thus in the meantime exist with some little comfort
and independence.

The next morning, having packed up his clothes, he
left a letter to his sister on the table in the sitting-
room of the little cottage to which they had removed,
detailing his intention, and what he had done for her
support, and bidding her and his aunt farewell. He

then, with an almost breaking heart, hurried from
the door. Carrying his portmanteau on his shoulder,
he walked some way to meet the coach going to London,
where he purposed first to look out for employment.
Weary and tired, he arrived there the next day, and then
began to consider what he should do. He had already
written to the few friends he possessed for introductions to people who might be of service to him in the
metropolis. Some paid no attention to his request,
others forwarded the introductions to the address he
fixed on, but few expressed any great regret at his loss.
At last, having received the letters, he set out to deliver them, but most of the people on whom he called
were from home, and the rest asserted they had no
means or influence to assist him. He then offered his
services in various directions, and in various capacities
for which he thought himself fitted; but from all those
to whom he applied he received the same answer—the
truth being, that in London there are always thousands
of young persons needing situations, so that a new-
comer cannot, or ought not, to expect an opening for
his services merely on making himself known. Besides,
Henry had never been previously employed; and this
of itself was enough to prevent him from being taken
into any house of business.

Too proud to descend, as he considered it, to any
humble kind of employment, and, perhaps, with recol-
lections of the smart appearance of the hussars of
his native town, he enlisted in the service of the East

India Company. A hurried and half-frantic note to
his poor sister only informed her that he was about
to leave the country for some time, and that she must
not be alarmed if she did not hear from him for several
months.

It appears to be customary for lads to change their
names when they enlist. According to the feelings of
educated Englishmen, there is a degradation in becoming a common soldier—a being sold, it may be said, for
the best years of life to a state of privation, and with
the most slender hopes of improvement in circumstances.
Following this practice of entering the army under a
feigned name, young Halliday called himself Hall, and
Hastings adopted the name of Hardy.

IV.

Such were the two youths whom circumstances had
degraded from their position, to be soldiers, bound for a
foreign clime. We left them walking on one of the
higher decks of the vessel. What was their conversation?

" A day or two more, and we shall reach St. Helena,"
observed Hardy; " and our next move will be glorious
India. Think of that, my dear fellow. Then for our
first campaign, when we may hope to plant our feet on
the steep ladder which leads to fame. Does not your
heart beat quick in anticipation of the moment when,
called from the ranks, an ensign's commission is the
reward of some gallant deed? How better far it is to

feel that you have the power to carve out your own fortunes, instead of being beholden to the ungracious assistance of relations, or the cold charity of strangers!"

Hall looked earnestly at his friend for some time. "Hardy, I envy you," he said at last. "You always contrive to conjure up some bright vision of the future, while I can never look beyond the dark realities of the moment. I have sometimes thought that I should like to tear aside the thick veil which shrouds my fate, but no sooner has the idea occurred, than an indescribable horror has seized me, and, shuddering, I have plunged into some scene of excitement to drown the dreadful thought."

"I am too little versed in philosophy to account for the feelings you describe," returned Hardy; "but I should think it is one you might by determination conquer."

"Conquer it! I do. I trample it under foot. I defy its suggestions. But in spite of me, it will rise again and again during the moments of solitude or inaction, till I feel a fierce delight in dwelling on it."

"Such are the freaks fancy often plays us," replied his friend. "You are suffering from some cause you are not aware of, which affects your spirits. To-morrow will dissipate it probably."

"To-morrow!" muttered Hall. "It is the tomorrow I dread. Sometimes I fancy that I shall never see our land of promise—India. Hardy, I would give thousands to know that I was to die bravely fighting

amongst a host of enemies. But that I scarcely expect.
I am a victim of desponding feelings. However, no
more of that. We shall see what to-morrow brings
forth."

The morrow came. The glowing sun arose from his
ocean bed, and directly ahead of the majestic ship ap-

peared St. Helena's lone rock, rearing the lofty heads
of its rugged peaks high above the blue waves, which
now leaped joyously at its base. To those long accustomed to gaze alone on the wide expanse of sea and the
canopy of heaven, the dark rock, towering above the
tall masts of the ship, appeared like some dreadful

monster ascending from the ocean's unfathomed depths to destroy them. First rose to view the barren slopes and crags of the north side of the island, with the great Barn Rock and the cone of Flagstaff-hill, cold, rugged, and bare; but on a nearer approach, green fields, trees, and plantations showed that the land was not quite a desert. Next were descried the church and houses of James Town, in their narrow valley, flanked on every side by strong batteries, and backed by a dark mass of woods. Coasting close in with the wall-like side of the island, a few tacks were made to reach the harbour, and the Indiaman dropped her anchor before the town, under the guns of the forts. Scarcely had they arrived, when an order came on board to disembark the troops and their baggage, and to march them up to the barracks.

"What can this mean?" inquired Hardy of his friend as they were buckling on their knapsacks.

"Mean!" exclaimed Hall; "that we are doomed to remain on this horrid rock till some other dupes come out to relieve us. I feared it would be so, but I hoped we might escape the punishment."

This information was correct. The recruits took up their quarters in the barracks, and in three days, their place on board the Indiaman being supplied by a few companies of well-disciplined and fully-accoutred troops, she sailed on her voyage, to the great indignation of a considerable number of the young men. That ship never reached her destination. Whether she sunk

beneath the ocean waves, was stranded on some distant
shore, or was destroyed by fire, was never ascertained,
for not a soul remained alive to tell her fate. Had the
catastrophe been known, it might have proved an important lesson to those who murmured at their lot; but
such was not to be. Constant drills, parades, mount-
ing guard, and other military duties, formed the daily
routine, while the most rigid discipline was maintained
among the men. The slightest fault was punished
with unwavering severity; the halberts were in constant requisition; and too many were exposed to the
ignominy of the lash. Hall and Hardy had hitherto
escaped punishment. Their good conduct and attention to their duties seemed to place them above the
chances of it; but this very circumstance seemed also
to excite the animosity of their captain more particularly against them.

It is to be hoped that there are not many such beings
in the world as Captain Pieman; but some few there
are, unhappily, both in the army and navy—the blight
of those who serve under them—who take an actual
delight in spiting the best men. "Eh, eh," said Captain Pieman one day to Hardy on parade, "you think
yourself a fine fellow, I know; a bit of a gentleman,
eh? But I'll catch you tripping one of these days, and
your dainty skin shall smart for it—so look out, my
lad." Hardy bit his lip, but he knew his duty too
well to answer a word to this brutal speech. Hall,
who was near him in the ranks, heard the words: his

eye flashed with fury, and he looked as if he would have sprung from his post and destroyed the petty tyrant. The captain, as he glanced along the ranks, observed the expression of his countenance. "I mark you, sirrah," he cried; "take care, or you will find the cat and your shoulders acquainted before long." Hall answered with a look of defiance, and from that moment he and his captain knew each other as deadly foes.

Week after week passed away; the cat did its work, and the recruits learnt their drill; whether or not the punishment made them better soldiers, was afterwards to be proved. At length they began to look forward to being quickly relieved, and complaints became general at their long delay on the island. This feeling was still further increased by seeing several ships with soldiers pass on to India, and by a rumour that the regiment was to be detained permanently on the island. Not long before this, the troops in St. Helena had broken out into open mutiny, when some of the men, led on by a sergeant, attacked the castle, a building on the sea-wall, where the governor was residing, and entering his apartments, hewed him to pieces with their swords. As soon as they had perpetrated the murder, they embarked in some boats they had secured, and succeeded in getting on board an American ship, which conveyed them safely to the United States, where they were numbered among the citizens of the republic. Notwithstanding this dreadful circumstance—for the mutiny originated from the same cause as the present dissatisfaction—the like system was pursued, the only difference being a stricter discipline and more constant watchfulness than had hitherto been exercised.

Some months thus passed wearily and grudgingly on, and the tyranny of Captain Pieman became insupportable. He had succeeded in his diabolical vow of bringing most of the men under his command to the halberts, but the two friends had hitherto escaped his malice. At last Hall, grown discontented and unhappy at the state of inaction in which he was kept, resorted to the dangerous expedient of drowning his cares in liquor, and was before long detected by his captain in a state approaching to intoxication. Condemnation to be flogged soon followed. Hall bore the infliction of his sentence with unflinching fortitude, but the feeling of his degradation entered into his soul. He could not recover his spirits; the gaiety of his manner had gone for ever. He became sullen and morose; nor could his comrades, who were hardened to the punishment, and could not comprehend his feelings, rouse him to activity.

In the meantime Hardy, who, by his excellent conduct and rapid progress towards a perfect knowledge of his military duties, had won the respect of all his officers except Pieman, was to have been made a corporal, and his future advancement was prognosticated by many, when an event occurred which blasted these brightening prospects.

V

One day when Hardy's turn to relieve guard was not
to come round till the evening, he left James Town, to
enjoy a short ramble over the island. He wandered on
for miles, thoughtless of how time sped. The sun and
the surrounding heights served him for landmarks, and
he felt certain that he could not lose his way; but
unexpected circumstances combined against him. His

watch had stopped, so he mistook the hour; suddenly
clouds collected round the summit of Diana's Peak;
the sky was overcast, deluges of rain came down; he
ran for shelter beneath a rock; his landmarks were
obscured, and he lost his way. He wandered about
without being able to find it; darkness came on, increasing his difficulties; and it was not till late at night

L

that, hungry and tired, he reached the town. The first person he encountered on approaching the barracks was Captain Pieman, who was returning tipsy from a party.

"What soldier is out of bounds at this hour?" asked the captain in his usual harsh tones. Hardy gave his name, and explained the cause of his irregularity.

"Oh, that's the reason, is it—eh? Let me tell you, my fine fellow, these excuses will not go down with me. Here, sergeant of the guard, keep this man under arrest," he called out.

"I speak the truth, Captain Pieman," urged Hardy in a respectful tone.

"What! You dare contradict me?" exclaimed the exasperated officer. "You shall pay for this to-morrow, depend on it."

Hardy uttered not another word, but, as he was marched off by the guard, he heard the captain vowing vengeance on his head. He passed the night in a miserable state, but his conscience was clear of wrong, and he hoped that, on giving an explanation of the circumstances, he should be acquitted. With the morning, however, came an aggravation of the difficulties of his position; for a report reached his ears that a robbery had, during the evening, been committed on a farm-house in the neighbourhood of James Town by a party of men, among whom a soldier of the garrison had been observed. The result of the investigation may have been anticipated. The charges of neglect of duty, in-

subordination and insolence to a superior, were proved.
The lofty-minded, romantic, and delicately-nurtured
Hardy was condemned to receive a hundred lashes;
and though no proofs of his having been concerned in
the robbery could be adduced, the stigma of suspicion
remained attached to his name. The following morning was to see the consummation of his misery and
disgrace, and as he lay on his rough pallet in the
dark room which served as the prison of the barracks,
how bitter were his thoughts, how acute the anguish
of his mind! "Have all my bright aspirations come
to this?" he mentally exclaimed. "Do thus end all
my hopes of glory? From henceforth to be pointed at
as a disgraced man, whose back is scored with the lash :
to be suspected of theft! Death were surely preferable!
Can I possibly endure it, and live?"

His spirit and frame were both alike exhausted by
the contention going on within, and he sunk at length
into a disturbed slumber. He had not slept long, when
he started, from feeling a hand placed on his shoulder,
and looking up he beheld the face of Hall gazing
earnestly at him, his features stern and fierce. An
officer's cap was drawn over his eyes, and a cloak was
thrown over his shoulders, beneath which appeared his
side-arms and a brace of pistols, while in his hand he
carried a dark lantern. Placing his fingers on Hardy's
lips, to impose silence, he made signs to him to follow.
Hardy mechanically obeyed; for so confused were his
senses that he had no time to reflect on what he was

about to do.   As he passed the door, he saw no sentinel
to oppose his progress, nor at a second post did any one
appear.   At the end of a passage a window stood open,
looking over the edge of a cliff.   Hall now, for the
first time addressing him, whispered in his ear that a
rope-ladder was secured to the sill, by which he must
descend.   " Hold on tightly, and never let go till you
find your feet on firm ground.   There's not a moment
to lose, as you value my life and your own; if you do
not, you destroy me, for I can tell you I will never be
taken alive."

Hardy felt the appeal, and did as he was desired.
Descending the rope ladder through the pitchy darkness, his hands knocking against the rough cliffs, not
knowing where he was to find himself, with the risk
every instant of discovery, he reached the bottom,
where he was soon afterwards joined by Hall, who
hurriedly informed him that they were outside the
fortress, with a path before them leading down to the
water's edge.

" I have no time for explanations," answered Hall
to Hardy's eager inquiries.   " Trust to me, and you
are safe.   A boat is in readiness to carry us beyond
the reach of our enemies.   Come on."

With these words he seized his comrade's hand, and
led him rapidly onwards.   They proceeded thus for
half a mile or more along a narrow track by the side
of the cliff, till, descending, they heard the ripple of
the water on the rocks close to their feet, and turning

an angle of the cliff, perceived a boat, with several men
in her, in a little bay, on the shore of which they stood.

"All's right," said Hall. "And now, Hardy, I
have done my duty to you. I have an affair of my
own to attend to; I would not miss it for the wealth
of India, which was once to be ours." And he uttered
a low laugh. "It will cause some delay, but that
cannot be avoided. The men cannot go without me,
for they do not know how to navigate the boat: you,
therefore, Hardy, must act as their captain. If I do
not return within an hour, stand off in a south-westerly
course, till you calculate you have run out of sight of
the island: the others will explain the rest. Now
step into the boat; keep all silent. Good-bye."

Saying this, he made Hardy take his seat in the
stern-sheets of a large boat, and hurrying off, was immediately lost sight of in the darkness.

A few words must serve to explain the cause of
Hardy's liberation. Some evenings before, while
drinking in a tavern with some of his comrades, Hall
had encountered the master of an American merchant-
man, who persuaded him and the rest to run off with
a boat, promising to pick them up in his brig when out
of sight of land, at an appointed spot, and to carry
them to America. Hall, determining not to leave his
friend behind, made arrangements to free him, which,
as we have seen, were thus far successful. He then
hurried back, at the risk of his life, to wreak his
vengeance on Captain Pieman, who he knew was living

in a remote part of the barracks by himself. What was
the nature of the injuries he inflicted may perhaps
be afterwards mentioned. It is sufficient here to say
that he added another to his already accumulated
transgressions.

VI.

Some time had elapsed after Hardy found himself
seated in the boat before his senses were sufficiently
collected to enable him to consider, with any approach
to calmness, the act he was about to commit. He was
on the point of becoming the character which of all
others a soldier detests the most—a deserter. True,
he was a prisoner, unjustly condemned to suffer an
ignominious punishment, and suspected of a crime
from which his soul revolted ; but notwithstanding all
this, he doubted whether he had a right to desert his
colours, to abandon his country, and to become the
citizen of another, often at enmity with his own. He
knew full well that no sophistry could extenuate the
step he was taking; but he had been led to adopt it
whilst smarting, in anticipation, under the disgrace of
a punishment against which every manly feeling revolted. The step had been taken, and it was now too
late to retract.

His thoughts wandered back to the home of his
childhood, to the boyish liberty he had enjoyed under
the paternal roof. And what was he now ? An
outcast ; at best entering upon a life hateful to

an honourable mind. He could no longer console himself with the reflection that, happen what might, he had performed his duty; from henceforth he would be ashamed to meet the eye of a Briton; no more could he see the land of his birth and his dearly-loved sister, but he was an exile wanderer among strange people. The thought was anguish. After waiting some time, the other men began to be alarmed at the non-appearance of Hall, and to express in low murmured tones their dissatisfaction at the delay. Chagrined at the detention, they had already made a pull from the shore, when Hall appeared, and they returned to take him on board. As soon as the boat touched the rocks, Hall sprang into her.

"The last time my feet shall touch that sterile shore; and now give way. When we are clear of the land, we will make sail. I am sorry for having detained you, but I am avenged;" and with a low hysterical laugh he threw himself back in the stern-sheets of the boat, and grasped the helm. "Give way!" he cried; and the men bending to their oars, the boat turned again from the shore.

The night was most lovely. There was no moon, but myriads of stars glittered in the dark-blue firmament, and reflected their light upon the mirror-like waters, while, sheltered by the lofty cliffs, the north-westerly wind which blew scarcely rippled their shining surface, and as the boat clove her way through them, urged on by the fear-impelled arms of the soldiers, her track was marked by a bright phosphorescent light, which played also round the bows, and on the oar-blades as they were dipped in beneath it, scattering a shower of drops, sparkling like diamonds, as they rose above it. Ahead of the boat was the boundless expanse of ocean; behind her arose, dark and frowning like some mighty demon of the waters, the towering cliffs of St. Helena.

For some time not a word had been uttered. "What are we about?" said Hardy, at last breaking silence.

"We are escaping from slavery and tyranny, and going towards a land of freedom."

"I wish I could persuade myself that we had done right," said Hardy.

"Nonsense!" answered Hall in an angry tone. "Regrets are ill-timed. Think what you would have had to undergo this very morning had you remained."

Hardy was silenced, but not convinced that he was acting rightly. The other six men whom Hall had persuaded to desert with him were discontented characters, most of whom had undergone frequent punishment—men with little or no education or sensitive feelings, but daring and fearless, and fit for any hazardous exploit. They had all come provided with arms, determined, should any boat be sent in chase of them, to resist to the last. They knew the danger of their undertaking, and every instant they fancied they could distinguish some vessel in pursuit, but each time the sail they conjured up faded from their sight. Then they declared they could hear the splash of oars in the distance, and redoubled their efforts, Hall encouraging them; for he knew full well the hot pursuit that would be made when their escape was discovered.

A fresh breeze springing up, they hoisted their lug-sail—the only one with which the boat was furnished—and laying in their oars, ran quickly down towards the spot where the American captain had undertaken to pick them up. As the morning broke, the rock of St. Helena appeared like a speck on the ocean; while shortly afterwards, between them and the land, the white canvas of a tall ship glanced in the beams of the rising sun.

"We are fortunate," exclaimed Hall, as his eye caught the welcome sight. "Our friend is better than his word. He promised to be up with us by mid-day, and we shall be on board him long before that."

"He must have got under weigh before daylight to be where he is," observed Hardy, who had been intently watching the sail.

"Mayhap she is some craft sent to look after us?" said Jackson, one of the most intelligent of the party.

"No, no; she's the American, depend on it," persisted Hall.

Hardy had for some time kept his eye on her. "She is not standing this way at all," he exclaimed; "she is beating up for the island, depend on it."

"Well, then, we shall have to wait rather longer than we expected," said Hall.

"No matter, we've plenty of food on board; and so, shipmates, to breakfast say I," exclaimed Jackson. "My pull has sharpened my appetite, I can tell you."

The proposal was acceded to without a dissentient voice, and the deserters set to work on their slender stock of provisions, and feasted merrily.

"We've enough victuals for three or four days," observed Jackson; "and as the American skipper undertook to provide us with food, I see no use in hoarding them up."

"The brig may possibly be detained for a day," said Hall, who had his reasons for not wishing to expend their provisions too rapidly. "The captain told me so the last time I saw him; but if it were to come on thick, you know he might be some time in picking us up."

The rest of the men, without inquiring further, promised to be more economical in future, and stretched themselves as well as they could along and over the thwarts to go to sleep. But neither Hall nor Hardy could rest. They pondered on the hazard of their present undertaking, their punishment and disgrace if captured, the hardships they must endure should the American miss them—perhaps their complete destruction. Should they even succeed in reaching the United States, could they hope to be received by honourable men in the rank of society to which they aspired? Their eyes were constantly turned towards the small speck in the horizon from whence the friendly ship was to come, but not a sail appeared. The sun rose high in the sky, his burning rays darting down on their unprotected heads; he reached the meridian, and gradually again descended towards the west, but no succour appeared. The men awoke one after the other, and lazily lifting up their heads, inquired if there were any signs of the American, but hearing that not a sail had appeared, again went to sleep. Thus passed the day; but when the sun was seen to dip beneath the waves, the whole party roused up, and again attacked the provisions, wondering what cause could have delayed the promised succour. Hall's statement, however, satisfied them, and they prepared to pass the night in the best way they could. He and Hardy were now at length overcome with fatigue and anxiety, and Jackson undertaking to keep a look-out, they threw themselves down to snatch a few hours' sleep.

Hardy slept soundly, and awoke refreshed; but as Jackson watched his comrade's features by the dim light of the stars, they appeared frightfully distorted, as if in agony: his hands frequently clutched convulsively at the air, and deep groans and broken exclamations escaped his bosom. Jackson was a brave fellow, but when Hardy awoke, he told him that he was frightened to look any longer at Hall, and could not go to sleep for thinking of what he had seen and heard. Again the glorious sun arose, and once more the deserters' eyes were gladdened by the sight of a sail about three miles off between them and the land.

"Here she is at last!" cried Jackson. The exclamation aroused Hall from his sleep. He sprung up on the after-thwart, and looked anxiously out. His gaze was long and steady; then dropping his hand, he sunk down again into his seat. "No!" he exclaimed; "she is a schooner, and beating up for the island. She must have passed us in the night."

Disappointment sat on every brow, and groans burst from the lips of some at their ill luck. "Not the brig!" ejaculated Hardy. "The American has played us false," cried one. "The villain! to entice us out here to let us starve," exclaimed another. Such were the expressions which went round from mouth to mouth for some time, till as the sun, rising higher in the sky, cleared away the mists of the early morn, the man who first made her out uttered a shout of joy, "The brig—the brig!" he exclaimed.

"If she is the brig, she is more lofty than the American," observed Hall, after watching her attentively for some time. "I suspect she's the *Firebrand* brig of war, which came into harbour two days ago, and that she is sent to look after us."

On hearing this opinion, consternation took possession of the hearts of most of the men.

"Well, what are we to do, Hall?"

"Keep out of her sight in the best way we can," he answered. "There is no great difficulty in doing so. If we stand away to the northward till the brig of war passes this, and then if we lie close when she comes any way near us, a hundred to one she steers within a mile of us without making us out."

"But suppose the American should not find us, what is to become of us?" urged one.

"For my part I'd rather the man-of-war picked us up than run the risk of starving," observed another.

"And be shot for deserters!" exclaimed Hall. "Mark me! you said you would stand by me if I would assist you to escape. I have kept my word; and the first man who attempts to signalise the king's ship, I will shoot him dead. I care not what happens, for I have determined never to fall alive into the hands of our tyrants. You know me, my friends, by this time, and may guess that I am likely to keep my word."

This speech silenced for a time the open discontent of the five men; for neither Hardy nor Jackson had made any complaint, and were rather inclined to side with his propositions. The lug was accordingly hoisted, and, close-hauled, they stood away to the north, increasing the speed of the boat with the oars. Hall had taken the precaution on the night of starting to have the boat painted on the outside with white, so that she might appear at a little distance to be merely the sparkling foam on the summit of a wave—a device to which he had often seen the smugglers resort to escape detection. Onward came the ship, her topsails and courses appearing one after the other, as if rising from the waves. She steered directly towards the spot where they had been but just before. Hall and Hardy watched her movements with intense anxiety. Should she be looking for them, what chance had they of escaping the vigilance of her active crew? and probably, they thought, her boats would be sent out to scour the ocean in every direction round. "We must lower the sail, and keep ourselves close, or we shall be seen," said Hall. "Now remember my hint!"

The sail was accordingly lowered, and the men, sitting down at the bottom of the boat, peered over the gunwale towards the man-of-war. For some time she stood steadily on, then suddenly altered her course to the northward. They gave themselves up for lost; but she might not yet have seen them. Hall drew his pistols, and examined their priming. Hardy endeavoured, speaking in a low whisper, to deter him from his purpose of not surrendering with life; but in vain. His proposals drove him almost to madness. Hardy himself felt almost resigned to his fate. He wished not to live, but his religion taught him to fear to lift his hand against himself. As the last moment of liberty seemed to approach, all held their breath in an agony of suspense. In an instant there was a revulsion of feeling. The brig of war suddenly altered her course; her sails were braced sharp up on the larboard-tack, and away she stood to the eastward.

VII.

The retreat of the vessel, which, going before a fresh breeze, was soon out of sight, caused the deserters

to congratulate themselves on their narrow escape.
They now took their morning meal, for they had been
too much occupied to think of eating; and then again
hoisted their sail, and ran back to the spot where they
expected the American brig to pick them up. Their
eyes followed the ship as she stood away to the eastward, till she was lost in the distance; but whether
she was in search of them or not, it was impossible to
say. All day they watched eagerly, scanning the line
of the blue sea, which seemed to cut across the peaks
of the far-distant rock, but no sail appeared above it
to cheer their hearts. Slowly the day dragged on; the
deserters attempted to lighten the time by conversation,
but a few sentences only were exchanged: they were
too anxious to talk. The evening closed like the
former one—in bitter disappointment. The night
passed in anxious doubts and fears, and another sun
rose over the heads of the misguided men. In vain,
as soon as light came over the world, they scanned the
horizon for the wished-for ship: not a sail dotted the
sea. All was blank and dreary. The eyes of the rest
were turned towards Hall with reproving glances. He
knew their thoughts, and felt the silent and merited
reproof. He saw that some strong measure must be
taken, or they would remain there till almost starved;
and then they would be compelled to return to the
island.

"Comrades!" he said, "I can no longer doubt that
some accident has prevented the American from sailing.

Perhaps some one has given information to the governor
that the captain was to pick us up, and if so, when he
does sail, his movements will be watched, and we shall
be taken to a certainty if we remain longer here. What
say you ?"

"What Hall says is very likely to be true," observed
some of the men to each other.

"Why, it is likely enough; but where shall we go?"
they asked.

"I have already said that I, for one, would never
return alive to St. Helena: but I have to make a pro-
position, to which I hope all will agree. Some distance from this there is, to the north-west, an island
called Ascension (he was afraid to say how many hundred miles). It is very small, but as it rises high out
of the sea, it can be observed at a long distance off.
The shores abound with fine turtle, which are very easy
to catch, and we shall be able to procure all sorts of
food to recover our strength, for we must live on short
commons till we get there; and we shall there also be
able to lay in a store of provisions to carry us over to
America, if we cannot find a ship bound in that direction. Are all agreed?"

The men consulted for some time together, and at
last came to the resolution of agreeing to what Hall
proposed. It must be remarked that, from the first,
both Hall and Hardy had taken that position which
their superior education and intelligence claimed. and
had been looked on by the rest in the light of officers,

though no formal respect was paid to them as such. Before shaping their course for Ascension, they examined into the state of their provisions, when they found that, with the strictest economy, eating merely enough to sustain life, they should have sufficient to last them for a week or ten days, by which time Hall calculated they would reach Ascension.

"Now remember the risk we run should it come on to blow!" said Hall. "I don't want to conceal it from you, but for my part I prefer death to slavery."

"So do we all," exclaimed the rest. "Then on to Ascension!"

The sail was hoisted, Hall took the helm, and shaping their course, the ill-fated boat stood away for Ascension. The weather proved uncommonly fine, and the wind shifted round more to the westward, so they made good way through the water. Besides Hall, Hardy and Jackson were the only hands who could steer by compass, so that they were obliged to relieve each other; and this giving them occupation, prevented them from dwelling so constantly on their condition. The other men passed most of their time asleep at the bottom of the boat; but it was dreary work, and soon they began sensibly to feel the want of their accustomed food and the scarcity of water; for Hall, who well knew that their only chance of living was by maintaining the strictest discipline, kept all the provisions in the after-part of the boat, serving out the daily rations with the greatest care. Day after day was the same: around

M

them the heaving, sparkling sea; above, the deep blue
sky and the hot sun, which, darting his fierce rays on
their heads, seemed to scorch up their very life's blood.

Six long days had thus passed. The seventh came,
and Hall asserted that on the morrow Ascension would
be in sight. The dawn of the eighth day arrived: every
eye, bloodshot with the heat and glare of the sun, was
strained to the utmost, as the light increased, to catch
sight of the wished-for shore; but they looked in vain
—no land was to be seen; and with cries of disappointment, they sunk down in their seats.

"We must have come along slower than I thought
we had," said Hall, anxious to encourage the rest,
though dreadful misgivings crossed his own mind.

"Can we have passed it?" said Hardy to him in a
whisper.

He answered with a look which showed that in his
own bosom he thought the suspicion correct. "To-
morrow we must reach the island," he exclaimed aloud.
"We will run on all day, and lay to at night."

They did as Hall proposed, but no appearance of land
cheered their sight that day; and the scanty remainder
of their provisions would only support their lives three
or four days longer. That night passed as many others
had done: some of the men lay groaning at the bottom
of the boat with hunger; others blamed Hall for leading them into this dreadful predicament; while he,
when he closed his weary eyes in slumber, appeared
visited by the most appalling dreams. With a terrible

shriek he awoke, and starting up in the boat, gazed around with looks of the wildest horror.

"What has alarmed you, my friend?" asked Hardy, taking his hand.

"Nothing—nothing!" he answered unconsciously. "Did I say nothing? Was it a mere sleeping vision, or some dreadful reality? Oh, Hardy! tell me, my friend, did you see no one? Did you hear no words of terrific import? Oh no, you could not, or you would have felt, like me, inclined to leap beneath the dark waves, and so end my ill-fated life and all my woes together! But what am I talking about? I am wandering in my mind—speaking sheer nonsense;" and he broke forth into a wild hysterical laugh.

Hardy endeavoured to calm him, and as the dawn appeared his spirits became more tranquil; but with the returning light, despondency took possession of the bosoms of the rest, for all around was the boundless sea and the blue vault of heaven. No signs of land appeared on either side. They sailed on till noon, in the faint hope of yet reaching the island, when Hall, after consulting with Hardy, announced to his comrades his conviction that they must have missed it altogether. This information was received with sullen apathy by some, and fierce anger by others, each throwing the blame of what they had already suffered, and what they might have to undergo, on Hall. He bore their rebukes manfully.

"Of your own free will you came, and nothing have

I done without consulting you," he answered. "If you suffer, so shall I; and in no way have I fared better than you; bearing, too, all the care and responsibility on my own shoulders. I will not conceal the perilous condition we are in, but we have still a chance of falling in with a ship from some part of America, or we must endeavour to reach the coast of the new world in the best way we can. I put it to the vote. If anybody can propose a better plan, let him say so."

"I agree with Hall; such is our only chance," said Hardy.

"And I," said Jackson.

"And I—and I—and I," exclaimed the others; and their course was once more altered in the proposed direction.

VIII.

The most indifferent could not but feel the hazard of their position. Were they to the eastward of Ascension, they might still have some hopes of falling in with it; but if not, a run of many hundred miles was before them, with provisions barely sufficient to sustain life for the space of two days longer. Hall assured the rest that they were likely to fall in with some ship which would at all events supply them with provisions; but his tones contradicted his words. The severe privations to which they were subjected had begun to tell upon all the party except Hall, whose bold unflinching spirit seemed to defy their power; his mental energies and physical strength both remained unimpaired. He had in his pocket a small map of the world, by which he found that, steering due west, they should reach near some of the Portuguese settlements, either Pernambuco or Bahia, from whence he proposed that they should find their way to the United States. "Only let us get somewhere," said one of the men, "and then we'll talk of what we will do afterwards."

The men had become fretful and sullen for want of food, and of water they had barely sufficient to wet their parched tongues, for not a drop of rain had fallen to replenish their store of that precious article. What a scene of misery did the boat with its forlorn crew now present! Placed in the midst of the wide Atlantic, a world of unbroken waters all around, provisions and water gone, no friendly hand to save, and perhaps, worst of all, each of the sufferers was more or less oppressed with remorseful feelings. The sophistry which led them to desert was now seen in all its deformity. They felt that, having undertaken a duty by a solemn engagement, they were bound to have fulfilled it at all hazards. In short, the greater number wished they had never quitted St. Helena. But such wishes were now too late.

Another day came, and as the provisions were served out, the men saw that, before many hours more had passed, there would be nothing wherewith to satisfy their gnawing hunger. But why dwell on what must have been long foreseen? At last the day arrived when they were *without food.* Slowly, and in silence, they ate their last mouthful; every man shared alike, and then they gazed vacantly into each other's eyes, and thought of *the morrow.* That dreadful morrow came. The sun rose red and hot, scorching up the remnant of moisture which existed in the emaciated frames of the wretched men. There they sat in their places more like spectres than living men, while the boat ran buoyantly and gaily over the dancing waves, conveying them whither they scarcely knew, except yet deeper into the vast expanse of the desert ocean, where food there was none. Yes; they felt that it was conveying them to death—death in its most appalling form—death by famine. What mockery it seemed as the boat bounded onward, as the glorious sun shone from out of the pure blue sky, and the clear sea sparkled brightly in his beams! Hope itself became faint within the breasts of all.

Towards the evening of that day one of the men, with his dim staring eyeballs, observed something dark floating ahead of the boat; they steered towards it. "A turtle—a turtle!" was the cry. Eagerly they hung over the side of the boat to grasp it in their arms, while one attempted to strike it on the head, for they had no other means of catching it; but, like the phantom of a dream, ere they reached the spot it sunk from their sight, and with a cry of disappointment they fell back in the boat. Another and another appeared to tantalise their hopes; while now a troop of porpoises, with curved backs, would leap from the water, to remind them that abundance was on every side, but not for them. Then a flight of tropical birds would pass over their heads, but none approached within their reach. Their eyes were hollow and grim; their tongues were parched; their voices sounded faint; they glared at each other with a strange and terrific expression. What dreadful thoughts were now passing through their minds! Each man looked at his fellow in silence ominous of ill. The day ended with groans, and in tears passed the sad night. Hall's strength seemed unabated; Hardy also bore up, supported by a courage he knew not that he before possessed. Some of the men had been whispering together during the night. It was scarcely day. The cold pale light of dawn threw into deeper shade the hollows of their sunken cheeks and eyes; these gave tokens of their sufferings. They sat upright. A sepulchral voice called Hall by name. He started up from the slumber into which he had lately fallen while Hardy was steering: he looked wildly around.

"Who calls me?" he asked.

"Food—food!" was uttered by several of the men.

"There is none!" was the disheartening reply. Every one knew that this was the case. Again there was a prolonged silence.

"We must eat!" exclaimed one.

"There is no food!" again answered their leader.

"Then some one must die to feed us!" shrieked forth

a soldier with accents almost supernatural. No one answered this dreadful proposal. Each man seemed to be conning it over in his thoughts. Their hearts sunk within them—their breath grew thick. Suddenly an unearthly cry arose of "Lots—lots!" They said no more; each man fully comprehended the resolve of his neighbour. Again they sat staring at each other.

"I protest against it," cried Hardy. "Heaven may yet send us aid."

"And so do I," said Jackson.

"The majority are for it," exclaimed the rest.

"Be it so," said Hall in a solemn voice. "We might yet exist another day, but I will not vote."

"Food—food!" cried the others, glaring at those who opposed them. "If we cannot have it by fair means, we will by foul;" and they seemed as if they were about to rush on Hardy.

"You will not consent to wait?" said Hall.

"Food—food!" was the dreadful response.

Without again speaking, Hall cut a piece of rope into eight uneven lengths, and throwing them into a hat together, the dreadful ceremony began. Who could venture to paint the countenances of those wretched men?

"I suppose," said Hall, "he who draws the *shortest* piece of rope must suffer for the rest? Shall it be so?"

"Agreed—agreed!" cried the men.

The lots were accordingly drawn, each man looking

away as he dipped his hand in the hat. A loud cry
escaped from Hall's lips—he had drawn the shortest
length! An awful silence ensued. Then starting up,
and drawing a pistol from his belt, Hall broke into a
hysterical laugh. The true, the haughty spirit of the
man showed itself.

"Fools!" he exclaimed, "do you think I, who am
the strongest, with more of life in me than all together
possess, will die to save your worthless lives? He who
moves, that instant dies!" Then he stood firm and
strong in the stern-sheets of the boat, his weapons
pointed towards the heads of his comrades. They
cowered before him. Suddenly a new temper came
over him. Hurling his pistols from him into the deep
ocean, he sunk down into the bottom of the boat, and
hiding his face in his hands, his bosom heaved convulsively. Oh with what bitter anguish was his mind
racked! No one disturbed him. It might have been
a kindness had they slain him. Perhaps he expected
it. He thought of his misspent youth, his wild and
vicious career in early manhood, the anguish he had
caused his father's heart, the crimes he had committed,
the murder which was on his soul. Then the slaying
of his captain appeared in its true light. "And must
I die with all these follies and crimes unatoned for?"
he exclaimed to himself. "Must I leave the bright
world I enjoyed so much—to go where? Oh God, I
know not! And for what? To enable these men to
prolong their dull lives for a few hours. Oh Heaven

give me strength to bear my lot!" He prayed for
mercy. "And yet," he continued, "it was I who led
them hither: had it not been for me, they would not
have embarked; had it not been for me, they would
have given themselves up to the ship of war. Then
Heaven's retributive justice has overtaken me, and I
must bow to his stern decrees. I am the guilty one.
It is right that I should suffer; and God's hand was in
it when the fatal lot fell to my share."

Earnestly he prayed. Hardy knelt by his side, and
petitioned Heaven to send them aid. He offered up
prayers for the life of his friend, and registered a vow
that, should his be spared, he would deliver himself up
into the hands of the authority from whom he had
escaped, and undergo the punishment to which he was
sentenced.

Hall at length rose. "Hardy," he said, "I have
determined to bear my fate as a man. Should you
escape, and something tells me you will, visit my
father. Tell him I died repentant, and petitioning for
Heaven's forgiveness and his. Comfort the old man,
but say not how or why I died. This is my last will
and testament. Comrades, your pardon for what I have
brought on you; and now, Hardy, I will show you how
a noble Roman died. I learnt it at school, and little
thought I should have to practise it myself. 'Tis all I
remember." And he laughed faintly. "Take my
hand, Hardy. Farewell! Who would think that in a
few minutes I shall be the inhabitant of another sphere?

It is a dream too frightful to dwell on; and madness
will seize me if I dispel it not with the reality."

Tears started from Hardy's dim eyes; and while he
was yet vainly entreating the rest to defer the fatal
moment till another day, Hall drew forth a nail from
one of the seats, and throwing off his coat, he opened
the veins of both his arms. Hardy sickened at the
sight, and hid his face with terror. Drop by drop the
ruddy stream gushed forth, and soon the strength of
their youthful leader grew as weak as the rest. Hardy
saw not what followed. A convulsive sob struck his
ear. It was the departing spirit of his friend.

IX.

The reader must picture the scene which now ensued:
no pen could describe its horrors. Jackson had taken
the helm. The boat sailed on as before. The sun
arose in glorious brightness; and some of those who
then lived were never to see it set, for death in other
forms was busy with those hapless beings. Madness
had seized one, and ere his comrades could save him,
with a loud shriek he leaped into the waves, and sank
for ever. Another lay down and never rose again.
Their numbers were thinning fearfully. Still the rest
clung to life. Never had Hardy or Jackson passed a
day and night of more acute suffering and wretchedness:
gnawing hunger was tugging at their vitals; anguish of

heart; dark forebodings of what the future might produce.

The dawn was approaching, when, as Hardy was seated at the helm steering, his eyes, from weariness, scarcely able to distinguish the compass, he was aroused by a cry from Jackson, who had just then risen from the bottom of the boat, to relieve him from his dreary watch. He looked up, and his eyes piercing the gloom ahead, a dark object rose directly before them.

"Land—land! A high rock directly ahead of us!" shouted Jackson with a hysterical laugh. "Land— land—land!" and he almost leaped into the ocean in his eagerness to reach it. The cry aroused the rest from their brutal lethargy, and lifting up their heads, they gazed at the dark mass which towered above them.

"Stand by to haul aft the sheet, if we should have to bring the boat up in the wind," said Hardy. "Out with your oars, ready to pull her round in case we find ourselves among reefs."

Onward sailed the boat towards the wished-for object, when Hardy, who was keeping his eyes intently fixed on it, exclaimed, "That is no land—it is a ship!"

"A ship! Where are her sails, then?" exclaimed Jackson. "It looks to me like a rock."

"It is the hull of a large ship, but completely dismasted," answered Hardy. "I can see her rising and falling in the waves. We must be careful when we approach her, to avoid the spars and masts probably towing overboard."

"Ay, ay; we shall have time enough for that," said Jackson. But he was deceived in the distance by the uncertain light; for scarcely had he spoken, when the boat passed close under the counter of a large ship, without a mast standing, though free from any of the wreck of spars which Hardy expected to find. He and Jackson, uniting their feeble voices, hailed the ship; but no answer was returned. He then entreated the other men to assist in calling for aid; and all joining in reiterated shouts, endeavoured to rouse the attention of any who might be on board, but without eliciting a responsive hail from the crew of the ship. All was silent as death.

"We must get on board without assistance," said Hardy. "Are there no ropes hanging over her sides by which we may clamber on board?"

"I can scarcely make out in this light," answered Jackson; "but if we run close alongside we shall find out."

"We shall be swamped if we attempt it, without great care; we have not strength to fend off as she rolls over," observed Hardy. And this was apparent to a person of any nautical knowledge; for though, with an active crew, there would have been no difficulty in boarding the ship, to persons so completely exhausted as were all in the boat, in the uncertain light of the break of day, it was a hazardous and difficult experiment. The sea, however, was tolerably tranquil At each return of that long swell which continually agitates the bosom of the Atlantic, the vessel rolled from side to side, till her ports almost reached the water.

"Has she any drink on board, I wonder?" exclaimed one of the men, in a voice husky from want of water.

"She may have, probably," answered Hardy; "and if you follow my directions, we may be able to procure some; but if not, I will not venture alongside, for we should all be drowned to a certainty. Now listen to me; get out your oars, boat-hook, and stretchers, to push off as she rolls over. Do you, Jackson, go forward, and endeavour to hook on to the main chains; and remember, let only one at a time attempt to spring on board."

Without further delay, Hardy steered the boat alongside the ship, while Jackson, with a rope ready in his hand, made it fast to the main chains. Climbing up the lofty side, he was not long in finding ropes to assist the rest. Hardy, seizing one, with difficulty hauled himself on board; but one of the other men, in his eagerness to spring forward, missed his hold as the boat receded from the side, and, with a shriek of despair, fell head foremost into the dark water. The boat and the ship again met; his late companions looked for him in vain: he rose not again. The remaining two were safely drawn on board, and the boat being allowed to fall off at the end of a long rope, the party, reduced to four, stood on the deck of the ship.

The light of day was appearing in the east, but, exhausted with their exertions, the hapless beings had scarcely strength left to crawl in search of the food they hoped to find. Not a living being appeared on the deck; not a sound broke the solemn silence, except the never-ending splash of the waves as they washed the sides of the ship. Shattered spars, bales of goods, rigging, and sails, lay about the deck, over which it was difficult to find their way in the dark, and with one accord they threw themselves down amid the confused mass, to wait till daylight should enable them to commence a search for food. At last the light fleecy clouds which floated in the sky became tinged with red, and Hardy, raising himself up, crawled as well as his strength would allow him, to the after-part of the deck. As he passed on, he saw more than one ghastly human form pressed down beneath the superincumbent wreck, destroyed evidently by the falling spars. Others, then, had been sufferers like themselves on the desert ocean—perhaps guiltless, too, of crime. But hunger urged him to proceed in his search, though it was with a feeling of awe that he descended the companion-ladder leading to the main cabins. What might he there expect to see? Perhaps forms like those on deck dissolving into corruption. The cabin door was closed: he opened it. No one was there. It was large and handsome, richly ornamented with a shrine and the figure of a saint at the after-part, which at once betokened her to be a Spanish or Portuguese ship; but what attracted his

eager gaze more than all the signs of wealth which
surrounded him, was a red clay jar slung in one corner
of the cabin. He eagerly clutched it: it was icy cold
to the touch : and tilting it up, he poured a draught of
pure cold water down his parched throat. Oh what
delicious nectar it seemed! With a cry of joy he called
on Jackson to partake of the reviving fluid, as the latter
entered the cabin; and then discovering an open locker,
he drew forth a basket of broken biscuit and a piece of
salt meat, which, dry and mildewed as they were, appeared delicious morsels to the starving wretches.
Scarcely had they commenced eating, when the two
other survivors found their way below. Hardy pointed
to the water-jar; both rushed to it at once, and, mad-
dened by their burning thirst, one struck the other a
blow which felled him to the deck, while he, placing
his lips to the brim, drank till, with a deep groan, he
sank down by the side of his comrade.

Hardy and Jackson seeing what had occurred, without the power of preventing it, dragged themselves to
the spot where the two men lay, to render them assistance; but it was useless: the lives of both were ebbing
fast away, one senseless from the blow, and his murderer
suffering excruciating torment from the quantity of cold
water he had swallowed. The two survivors, taking
warning from their fate, partook but sparingly of the
food; and then, unable to move from the cabin, they
lay down, and a deep slumber fell over them. It was
towards the close of evening when they awoke,

with their burning thirst unassuaged; and on returning
to the water-jar to drink, the fate of their two comrades
was recalled to their minds by seeing them lying where
they had fallen, both with life extinct. They drank
and ate again; and then, overcome by excessive drowsi-
ness, threw themselves into berths on either side of the
cabin; nor did they again awake till the sun of another
day was rising from his ocean bed. Hardy arose with his
mental and bodily faculties strengthened and refreshed,
and collecting his thoughts, he felt how ungrateful to
Heaven he had been; then kneeling down, he offered
up his hearty thanksgiving to that Almighty Power
which had thus far preserved him.

Along with Jackson, he again partook of the provisions they had discovered; and then, with renovated
strength, set out on a tour of inspection through the
ship. They first clambered on deck, where such a
scene of havoc and confusion met their eyes as they had
rarely witnessed. On further examination, it was
evident that the vessel had been dismasted in a gale,
either at sea or on a lee-shore, where she had been
deserted by her crew. That the last was the case,
they discovered afterwards when going forward, from
seeing the remains of two cables hanging out of the
hawse-holes: so it was clear that after the crew had
left her, a strong wind had come off the land and driven
her out to sea.

The individuals whose bodies they saw had been killed
by the falling spars, and the condition they were in,

N

was sufficient evidence of the length of time she had
been floating untenanted on the ocean; for not a particle
of flesh remained on their bones, and it was their
ghastly skulls which had first, in the uncertain twilight,
caught Hardy's eye. At first it struck Hardy that they
might be able to navigate the ship to shore, or till they
fell in with another vessel; but, unaccustomed to a
seaman's resources, he soon found that this was beyond
their power, and as probably she would scarcely be able
to weather another gale, they prepared to resume their
voyage in their own frail, but easily-managed craft.
The boat, which had fortunately escaped injury by
knocking alongside for such a length of time, was now
hauled up, and they set to work to prepare her better
for sea, by nailing planks round her gunwale, and
decking over a considerable part forward, to shelter
their stores from the spray, covering it tightly over
with canvas. They then fitted fore and aft sails, and
filled all the smaller casks and jars they could find with
water, of which there was an abundance on board, stowing them at the bottom of the boat. Over this they
placed several casks of salt beef and pork, with others of
biscuits, covering all up with canvas, filling up the
spare room with wood for firing—having discovered
some iron work in the caboose, in which a fire could
safely be lighted. They also collected a supply of
clothes, carpenter's tools, and numerous other things
which they thought might be necessary. Having cooked
some food, sufficient to supply them as long as it could

last good, they shoved off from the ark which had proved their preservation.

Three days had passed since they first stepped on board the ship, for in their weak state all these preparations took up a considerable time; but as the weather gave every promise of continuing favourable, they felt it was better to complete everything which might be necessary to encounter any heavy gale to which they might be subjected. How fearfully had their numbers decreased! Of the eight who left St. Helena, two alone remained alive. Before leaving the ship, they wrapped the bodies of the dead in a torn sail, and with some heavy shot attached, launched them in their common coffin into the deep. What a contrast was there now between their condition four days ago and their present one! A fine breeze carried them onward; they had abundance of all the necessaries of life, and were daily recovering strength; but many days passed before their eyes were gladdened by a sight of land; and when at length their feet once more touched dry ground, they found that their trials were not yet over. After returning thanks to the Almighty Being who had thus far preserved them, they were walking towards a fort which they observed along the coast, when they found themselves surrounded by a party of Portuguese soldiers, who, roughly seizing them, dragged them before the commandant of the fort. Here they were unceremoniously consigned to a miserable dungeon, to await an investigation of their character.

X.

We now shift the scene of our story to St. Helena.
On the occasion of the desertion which has been
narrated, the fate of the unhappy men was not believed
to be doubtful. No sooner had the authorities notice
of their disappearance, than an embargo was laid on
all the ships in the harbour, with the hopes of compelling them to return ; and this it was which prevented
the American from keeping his promise. As, however,
they did not return, they were supposed to have perished

miserably. A new governor had been appointed, by whose enlightened, though strict management, a spirit of perfect subordination had been introduced among the troops under his orders. One day, about a year after the dismal events narrated, he was walking on a terrace overlooking the sea, in front of his residence, when a young man, in the costume of a sailor, presented himself before him.

"What is it you want, my good man?" said the governor.

"I come, your excellency, to fulfil a duty I owe to my country, and to accomplish a vow," answered the young man in a deep voice, slightly trembling with agitation.

"What is this? I do not understand you," replied the governor, thinking his visitor was affected in his mind.

"You see a man who has deserted from his colours, and has returned to deliver himself up to justice," said the stranger.

"A heavy offence, young man, and one which must be severely punished," said the governor.

"I am ready to undergo any punishment the laws of the service may inflict," said the stranger.

"You! What are you talking about? There have been no desertions since I came to the island, full ten months ago," answered the governor mildly. "But stay, young man," he continued, regarding him earnestly; "I never forget a countenance I have once seen, and those features of yours I know well. What is your name?"

"Hardy was the name under which I enlisted," answered the stranger.

"But not the one you always bore?" answered the governor, eyeing him still more attentively. "You say that you enlisted: in what corps, then? and how do I see you with the appearance of a seaman?"

"I assumed the dress because I acted as one to work my passage here," answered Hardy; and then, as rapidly as the governor would allow him with his frequent interruptions, he narrated all his adventures. How he had escaped from the Portuguese fort with Jackson; how he had reached Pernambuco; and, after numerous hardships, had arrived at Rio de Janeiro, from whence he worked his passage in an English ship to the Cape of Good Hope, and so back to St. Helena.

When he had concluded, the governor, instead of ordering him into instant confinement, calmly addressed him. "Your fault in deserting was a heinous one for a soldier; but in your case there are many extenuating circumstances, and you have already been most severely punished. Your conduct, too, in returning as soon as you had the power, in spite of all difficulties, and with the uncertainty of how you might be treated, is worthy of all commendation. This should be a set-off against all your previous faults, had we not the acknowledgment of that unhappy man, Captain Pieman, on his deathbed, that he had treated you most unjustly. I now remember all the circumstances, for I made full notes of them on my arrival. He even entreated that Hall might be pardoned, for he recovered from the wound inflicted by that unhappy man, and died only a few months ago from another cause. So far, I may congratulate you, young man, on your providential preservation; and now, tell me the name you bore before you enlisted—I have my reasons for wishing to know."

"I would rather it were never heard till every stain of dishonour had been washed from it," answered Hardy in a faltering tone.

"You are right; and if I mistake not, it is one as noble as any in the land. Your accents betray the station to which you were born. Do I mistake you?"

"Your excellency is, I firmly believe, correct; my name is Hastings."

"I thought so. Your father was my earliest friend, and often have I seen you during his lifetime. For his sake, as well as for your own, the first commission I can bestow shall be yours."

"Pardon me," exclaimed Hardy, scarcely able to express himself from emotion; "I am not ungrateful for the kind interest you show; but after what has occurred, I cannot accept your offer. I must win my way to the rank you would bestow, and not receive it as an undeserved gift. Then may I be able to lift my head among my equals, and defy the malice of my enemies!"

"I applaud your determination, and it shall be as

you wish. The eye of those with more power than I have shall be upon you; and if the chances of war allow it, your fortune shall be in your own hands. Farewell, Mr. Hardy; my heart is with you, though from henceforth you must assume the station you have chosen. A ship is expected shortly, to convey troops to India. You shall join them. In the meantime enlist again, and do your duty here under the name you have chosen."

The kind governor made a sign to Hardy to leave him; and the latter, with feelings of heartfelt gratitude, and a firm resolve to deserve his good fortune, forthwith went about the duties he had been ordered to perform. Hardy's return, and many of the circumstances connected with the fate of his companions, were well known at the time in St. Helena, though his real name never transpired.

XI.

Several years after these events, as Mr. and Mrs. Ravenhurst were seated one lovely evening in summer in the drawing-room of their beautiful villa on the coast of Devonshire, with their lovely children playing round them as they gazed forth on the moonlit dancing waters of the ocean, the servant announced a visitor.

"Who did you say?" asked Mrs. Ravenhurst. But before an answer could be returned, a stranger entered, and bowing to the master and mistress of the house, took the seat which was offered him.

"My intrusion at this hour may appear strange," he observed; "but I am anxious to make inquiries respecting a dear friend, a near relative of yours, I understand—Henry Hastings—Colonel Hastings, I ought to say."

A deep sigh escaped the bosom of the lady. "I once had a brother of that name," she answered; "an affectionate, noble brother. But he, we have too much reason to fear, has long been dead."

"And yet I can scarcely be mistaken," observed the stranger, as if musing. "We were in India together but a few months ago, and quitted it at the same time. He himself assured me of the relationship."

"Sincerely do I wish you are not mistaken," said Mrs. Ravenhurst. "It would indeed be an unspeakable increase to my happiness to have my long-lost brother restored to us."

"Did he tell you the reasons for keeping us so long in ignorance of his existence, sir?" said Mr. Ravenhurst, wishing to ascertain the truth of the stranger's statements.

"His adventures were romantic in the extreme, and having already given his sister cause to mourn his death, while every day the reality was so likely to occur in the chances of war, he was unwilling to give her the additional grief should he fall. That she was happily married to the man of her choice, he had heard, and he therefore determined to remain unknown till he had won the station and name for which he panted. You have seen, probably, the name of Colonel Hardy mentioned in the accounts of the late Sepoy insurrection in India?"

"Frequently—one of the most gallant and fortunate officers in the service!" exclaimed the husband and wife in the same breath.

"Such was the name your brother assumed," said the stranger in an agitated tone. Just then the servant entered with lights. Both Mr. and Mrs. Ravenhurst started, and gazed earnestly at the stranger.

"Henry!" exclaimed the husband, hastening towards him.

"My brother!" cried the lady, throwing her arms round his neck, and bursting into tears—but they were tears of joy. It was Colonel Hastings, once the deserter from St. Helena, now restored to home and friends; but few can tell the agony of mind and the physical suffering he endured before he once more trod the pathway to honour.

CIUDAD RODRIGO,

AND HOW WE TOOK IT.

BY A CHELSEA PENSIONER.

WHEN I belonged to the light company of the 52nd
Regiment, we lay before Ciudad Rodrigo, which is a
fortress in the northern part of Spain, not far from the
borders of Portugal. We were, you'll understand.

fighting the battles of the Peninsula, under Lord Wellington. He had made up his mind to turn the French out of all the fortresses on the frontiers, and then to drive them before him, right across Spain, into their own country. About eighteen months before, in July 1810, the French had taken Ciudad Rodrigo while our army lay not far off, but we were not strong enough to prevent them, and they had held it ever since. We again arrived at the place on the 8th of January, 1812, after a march of four days, from Martiago, in terribly severe weather, as bad as wind and snow and cold could make it. Our division crossed the river Agueda just before daylight; then we encamped on some high ground in front of the town. It was very severe work, for we had no tents, and there was not a twig in the neighbourhood to build a hut with, and little enough wood even for making our fires. So we slept on the bare ground, wrapped in our blankets, and when we awoke every morning we found ourselves covered thickly over with hoar-frost. We didn't mind it for ourselves; but the poor fellows who got wounded suffered much. As I was saying, we had marched from Martiago. For some miles before we got near Ciudad Rodrigo we had passed over a green plain, and at last we caught sight of the place we had come to take, built, it seemed, on some low rocks rising out of the plain, with the river Agueda flowing at their base, from the east towards the Douro. All the country round was flat and open, except a height behind which our army was posted, and from which Lord Wellington was then making his approaches.

Ciudad Rodrigo was, you'll understand, a walled town, but could scarcely be called a regular fortress, except for a work called a *fausse braie*, an angular wall which covered the ordinary walls of the town.

The first operation we undertook was to carry an outwork by assault. It was done in gallant style. The men told off for the purpose were divided into four parties. Three marched up to the three sides of the fort, and fired on every Frenchman who dared to show his head above the ramparts, while the storming-party, to which I belonged, got into the ditch, and, placing our ladders, up we climbed in spite of shells and lighted grenades, which were thrown down on our heads. Many of our officers and men were killed or wounded; but we gained a footing in the works and fought our way on.

Some of our party had been supplied with crowbars, and were to force the gate at the gorge at the rear of the work. Suddenly it was blown open, and in they rushed. The whole garrison was either bayoneted or taken prisoners, and the fort was won. How the gate was blown open was the wonder. I afterwards learned. A French artillery sergeant was in the act of throwing a live shell on the heads of the storming party in the ditch, when he was shot dead, and the righted shell fell within the fort. An officer seeing this, and fearing that it would explode among the men defending the parapet, kicked it towards the gorge, where it was stopped by the bottom of the gate. It there exploded and blew open the gate, as I have described.

We pushed on our advances as fast as we could. The army was in four divisions, and one relieved the other every day in the trenches. There was no time to be lost, for the French were advancing from all directions to relieve the place, and our object was to take it, so as to have all our force at liberty to fight them.

I won't say anything against campaigning and fighting a battle every now and then,—but that work in the trenches, in the middle of winter, with shot and shell and bullets rattling about one's head, I do say I don't think any man can like for itself. Still we cheerfully went through with what we had to do. When we were not on duty in the trenches we were put up under cover in the ruined villages in the neighbourhood, and when our tents arrived we were still better off. At last the batteries opened, and two breaches, a great and lesser breach, were formed. It was now a question whether the French would give in or stand an assault. Their flag still flew on the ramparts. Lord Wellington decided on storming the place. The third division, under Major-General Mackinnon, was ordered to assault the great breach ; the light division, to which I belonged, the lesser. While our officers were reconnoitring, so as to know their way up to the breaches in the dark, we were halted under shelter near a convent,

and there we waited, wishing that night would come
on One hundred men from each of three regiments,
the 52nd, 43rd, and 95th, had been allowed to volun-
teer to form the storming party. I was among them,
and we then found that a very brave young officer of
my regiment, Lieutenant Gurwood, was to lead the
forlorn hope. Who was to form it we did not know;
but all were ready enough, if called on.

As soon as it grew dark we moved to the rear of the
convent wall, and Mr. Gurwood then told off three
sergeants and thirteen file. I was one of them.
"Lads, you are the forlorn hope," said he; "all you
have to do is to follow me. We must make a lodgment
in the breach, and direct the column to it." We were
ordered not to fire, but to fight our way on with the
bayonet. We all stood ready—behind us the men with
ladders, axes, and hay-bags, and then the main body.
It was an awful time. Where might all of us be in a
few minutes? We waited for the signal—three guns
from the batteries. There they are! "Off" was the
word. Away we started. I kept close to our brave
young leader. We got ahead of the party carrying
the hay-bags intended for us to jump on, and so letting
ourselves down into the ditch where the ladders were
thrown to us, we ran on till we got close to the breach
in the outer work. The enemy had not yet discovered
our little party, but were directing their attention to
that breach alone. Instead therefore of pushing for it,
the ladders were placed against the wall on one side;

then up we scrambled, and, to the astonishment of the Frenchmen in the breach, took them in the rear, and quickly disposed of some of them, while others escaped towards the breach in the wall of the town. We followed. All this time our covering party were keeping up a hot fire over our heads, while fire-balls and grenades, and shot and stones, were being rolled down upon us by the enemy. In spite of all opposition, we fought our way up to the breach of the town, where, having made a lodgment, we gave a hearty shout to direct the column to it. We were not at the top though. "On, on," was the cry. Our way lay up a mass of crumbling stones, high and steep. As yet we hadn't fired a shot. Our leader ordered us to load. Up we scrambled. The enemy crowded at the top. Missiles of every sort were showered down on us, and though we shot some of the enemy, one and all of us were rolled back again to the bottom of the breach. Many were killed; our leader was wounded, but he was again on his legs; and more men arriving, once again we rushed upwards. With a loud cheer we gained the rampart; the enemy gave way. "The place is won," was the cry. Our men, British and Portuguese, poured in, for the Portuguese took their part in the assault, and behaved gallantly.

I was following our lieutenant to the left when we saw some of our people about to bayonet a French officer, who would not give up his money. The lieutenant sprang forward and saved the Frenchman's life.

The poor fellow was very grateful, and begged him to protect him further. Our lieutenant said he would, but that he must show him where the governor of the place was to be found. Away we went. The men of the light division were now pouring into the town, and the French garrison, in all directions, were crying out for quarter. I was a young soldier. I had never before been at the taking of a place by storm; but I saw sights that day, and did some too, which I don't like to think about. The opposition we had met with, and the cold and hardships we had gone through, had made us pretty nearly mad. We, that is to say, our lieutenant and those who still kept with him, at last reached the tower, where the governor and many of the French officers had taken shelter. At first they wouldn't open the gate, thinking they were going to be murdered; but our lieutenant promised them that he would protect their lives with his own. After some further talk the gate was opened, but we found that the governor was in a room inside. The door of this room was at last unbarred, and as we pushed in we saw that it was full of French officers. I thought that they were going to make a rush out and kill us; but instead of that, one of them, who was the governor, cried out that they surrendered, and handed his sword to our young lieutenant, who told him and the rest that he would do his best to preserve their lives. However, we succeeded in carrying the prisoners to Lord Wellington, and I believe not the life of one

o

of them was lost. Our loss was heavy. General
Mackinnon was killed, and General Craufurd died of
his wounds a few days afterwards; while about a
hundred other officers and men were killed, and more
than three hundred were wounded. During the siege
nearly four times that number had been killed or
wounded. We had plenty of fighting after that, when
I joined the hussars, and lost my arm at Salamanca.

FLAYED ALIVE.

Two young gentlemen were sitting in the inner room
of a pastry-cook's shop, at a marble table, with iced
creams before them, when a party of boys rushed into the
shop and began to regale themselves on Butter-Scotch.
One of the two young men within, recognising among
the new comers a pupil of the Grinder's Hall establishment, which he himself had only left a year before,

called out, "Holloa, Old Tongs, is that you?" to
which the lad, whose right name was Thompson, but to
whom the nickname had been applied from his reputed
resemblance in form to a pair of tongs, replied in
the same familiar manner, "Is that you, Ferguson?
I'm glad to see you." They shook hands, and this
lad's companions were introduced as the *last half lot* at
the Hall.

"I say, Mrs. Pye," said Ferguson, "I must stand
treat for these new ones at Grinder's. What will you
have, boys? Oyster pâtés, tarts, gingerbread nuts,
sponge cake, Bath buns, and ices : eat away, my chaps ;
this is the best sort of cramming and grinding, eh,
Tongs? Sit down here, next my friend Dickson.
Dickson, this is Mr. Thompson, *alias* Tongs."

This formal introduction over, the boys set to, determined to make the most of Ferguson's unlimited
order. Indeed, every one of the party showed a disposition to cramming, or more grammatically, to being
crammed : and Mrs. Pye gave many marks, after her
own method, to each of the juveniles engaged in the
competitive work at the counter. The business, on
the whole, was well and energetically executed, and a
respectable score attached to every name.

While the juveniles were concluding the measure-
ment of liquid and solid quantities by the rule of sub-
traction, Ferguson proposed this question—

"Who smokes?"

"I do! I do!" omnes respondent.

"Bene bene respondistis; digni estis intrare in nostrum—"

"Fumitorium," suggested Mr. Dickson, as they were retiring to a back room, where smoking was allowed.

There was some real smoking, and some affectation of it, and the box of cigars was breaking bulk, when Mr. Dickson, who had been smoking freely, but speaking little, asked if something of a horrible kind had not occurred, a few years before, at Grinder's Hall—something of murder under circumstances of atrocious cruelty?

Ferguson laughed heartily, as did Tongs also. After a few refreshing puffs, Ferguson said—

"I will tell you all about it. Just before I left Grinder's Hall, two of us had been reading, in an encyclopædia, the account of a hospital at Surat, founded for fleas and other insects, where, every night, some poor fellow allowed himself, for hire, to be strapped down and preyed upon by fleas and other voracious and venerated vermin. There was a queer chap among us, whom nobody liked, though he was quiet and harmless; a great feeder, and very lazy; and such a heavy sleeper, that it was sometimes almost impossible to awaken him. He seemed, when asleep, like one under the influence of chloroform, and would hardly wince if pins were stuck into him. Somebody proposed—"

"It was *you* yourself," interrupted Tongs.

"—That a lot of hungry fleas should be caught and corked up in a quill, and, when well starved, let loose to feed upon Heavyside's body."

"How were they trapped?" inquired Dickson.

"Oh! we managed this—with a little trouble, of course. We then put two score of the tribe into a quill, and fastened it at the opening by a bit of muslin, which admitted air sufficient to keep them alive. The next night, when they had great appetites, and our victim was in his deep sleep, one of the confederates—"

"Oh! Ferguson!"

"—Put out the candle, and placed the quill with its sanguinary occupants on the throat of poor Heavyside. We then gently took off the muslin curtain and left the blood-suckers to do their work. Next morning, when Heavyside awoke, he perceived that his body was punctured all over, and covered with bloody blotches. The fleas were found so gorged after their debauch, as to be easily taken into custody and put to death, else the bed-room would have become a pest to the house."

"How was this trick discovered?" inquired Dickson, laughing.

"Poor Heavyside was so feverish that the doctor was called in, and was puzzled beyond measure. He was going to rub him all over with mercurial ointment and confine him closely to his room, when one of the confederates, pricked by an accusing conscience—"

"Oh! Ferguson!"

"—Told the facts to the doctor, and he made our peace pretty well with Mr. Grinder. The best of it was that, in the *Lying Mercury*, it was reported that

' A YOUNG GENTLEMAN HAD BEEN FLAYED ALIVE at a well-known grinding establishment, not fifty miles from ——, and that the police were in active pursuit of the perpetrators of the atrocious crime.' "

"That is exactly what I heard," said Dickson.

A general burst of laughter followed.

"But still," said Dickson, "I cannot understand how this trick became so absurdly exaggerated. It must have been injurious to the character of the school."

"So it was; and poor Grinder was in an awful stew about the report.

'Magna sit fama per urbes.'

It originated in this way. We had an Irish writing-master, named O'Rourke, who pronounced *ea* in any word as *ay*;—tea, *tay*; pea, *pay*; sea, *say*; and flea, *flay*. In relating the fact, instead of saying that the boy was flea-bitten, or even flea-d, he, of course, without being conscious of the *équivoque*, very gravely reported that Master Heavyside had been *flayed* from head to foot by some of his own schoolfellows."

"And you were flogged, of course," said Dickson.

"I was condemned," said Mr. Ferguson, "to write a hundred lines, in clear and close penmanship, on the physiology of the flea."

"With statistics, I hope," observed Mr. Dickson, "to demonstrate his physical, social, intellectual, and sanitary conditions."

"Of course," replied the other, "I did not omit those considerations; nor other interesting facts, such as its appearance when about to glut itself with the blood of its victim, which I illustrated with a fancy sketch. Then I spoke of *nits*, and the important place thay hold in creation."

The affected seriousness of Mr. Ferguson set all the lads laughing. One of them, however, asked him, " What are nits ? "

" They are extremely minute eggs at first, which the mamma fleas deposit on the tender flesh of some unlucky living creature—suppose a cat, or dog, or pigeon—with a warm, cosy skin and hair, and whose flesh is fit to nourish the nits, transformed at first into worm-like insects, which, in about a fortnight, become lively and ticklesome. In a few days more they are metamorphosed into fully shaped and active fleas, playing hop, skip, and jump without any training. I was obliged to banish my poor Skye terrier, Puck, the other day, because a tribe of fleas had so multiplied in his matted curly hair, in spite of flea-powder, and washing, and combing, and so tortured him with their pincers, that he became an intolerable nuisance to me. Indeed the surplus population continually emigrating from his carcass to my clothes and bedding, and, of course, to my skin, would have devoured me, if I had not sent the poor brute away to a thick-skinned shepherd, into whose hide, I suppose, the fleas do not drive their lancets. I cannot say, with Horace—

'Ubi plurima *nit*ent in *corpore*, non ego paucis
    Offendar maculis :'

as I am acutely sensitive to flea-bites, and feel great disgust at the red and inflamed spots they occasion, which, viewed through a microscope, are terrific blotches of gore and wounds."

"Give us small change for that great Latin quotation," said one of the lads.

"Well, my version is—'Where nits (or fleas) abound, I don't grumble at a few flea-blots.'"

But to go on with Ferguson's school compilation. He told them that "the perfect flea, examined by the microscope, is by no means ugly. Its body is covered all over with black scales, curiously pointed and folded over one another, so as to yield to the nimble motions of the body. These scales are polished and furnished at the edges with short spikes, beautifully arranged."

"Ah," cried out Tongs, "I suppose that the construction of the knight's scaly armour, or coat of mail, which we see in the Tower of London, was suggested by a flea's coat."

"Well said, Tongs," responded Ferguson; "you are quite a conjuror for finding out things. Now that's clever! and here's a puzzle for you in return :—

"Why" (his expressive brow contracting and expanding as the brilliant thought was working within), "why is every flea—yes, why is every flea, as I have drawn him, a knight-errant by birth? Do you give it up? Because his knighthood (*nit*hood) is coeval with his earliest existence."

"Ha. ha. ha!" omnes.

"Will you let me finish my sketch?" asked Ferguson; who was allowed to conclude.

"A flea can jump, at one spring, two hundred times higher than the height of its own body, by means of the wonderful spring in its feet and legs. This, compared with a man's height of six feet, is as if a man could jump four hundred yards!"

"No wonder," said Tongs, "it is so terribly hard to catch a flea, which jumps so many inches from you, and slips away while you are trying to nab him with your forefinger and thumb."

"What sort of legs has a flea, and how many of them, Mr. Ferguson?"

"Six hairy legs, with several joints. Two of these protrude from the snout part; and between these forelegs is the lancet or sucker. The other four legs are joined at the breast, and folded one within another, ready for the spring, all at the same instant, which carries the jumper to such a wonderful distance."

"I should like to examine a flea in a microscope," remarked two or three of the boys.

"So you may, and dissect him," replied Ferguson, "in a drop of water. There you may discern the interior of his body, and the movements within."

"Is it true that the flea will not feed upon the dead or dying?" said Mr. Dickson to his friend.

"Certainly. It must have a living, warm, blood-circulating subject to fatten upon. I was about to say that, besides this, we were condemned by Grinder, who has no little fun in him, to work out the following problem. Listen, youngsters, *favete auribus:* 'If a flea, at one spring, jumps two hunderd times its own height, how many jumps must it make to travel one mile, three-quarters, and six perches?' Again, to another he gave this easier problem: 'With the above data, how many jumps must a flea make from a floor to reach the nose of a boy stretched on a bed three feet four inches higher than the floor?' But I remember a stiffener, which took us a week to solve: 'Supposing that one flea had sucked four grains of Heavyside's blood in nine hours, ten minutes, and three seconds, and that the thirty-nine other fleas had each sucked the same quantity in the same time; and supposing that all the blood in Heavyside's body amounted to six quarts, what number of fleas would be required to suck him dry in three weeks, two days, one hour, six minutes, and three seconds?' Another calculation ordered was, 'How many fleas would be required to draw a gun or carriage of a given weight, as exhibited by showmen?'"

This was a pleasant hour's chat, during which thirty shillings' worth of eatables and cigars was consumed. Who paid the bill? Mr. Ferguson nodded to Mrs. Pye, as much as to say, "Put that to my account;" but as this young gentleman, who had then but £100 a year, lived at the full rate of £300, it would have been very doubtful if Mrs. Pye and other tradespeople would ever have been paid by him, had he not, after this day's occurrence, put this problem to himself: "If I spend £300 in one year, and have only £100, how long will it take me to pay my debts?" Not being able to solve this problem so satisfactorily as in the cases of the fleas, he prudently resolved in future to make his expenditure square with his income.

As these young men and boys were going out of the shop, and other parties were coming in, two miserable children, apparently brother and sister, put out their thin hands, whispering, "Give me a halfpenny bun." They had been viewing the cakes and sweets through large plate glass, and longing for a taste of them. Poor children! perhaps they were very hungry—they looked half-starved; perhaps they had none to care for them; perhaps they groaned under the tyranny of a gin-drinking and brutal stepfather, or stepmother, who forced them to beg; perhaps they were timid and well-disposed children—good—with respect to their bad home-condition. "Charity hopeth all things," but Mr. Dickson spoke uncharitably. "Go along, you idle, thievish brats; go to school, or go to work." He had notions of political economy, and knew that alms given to beggars are a premium for the encouragement of mendicancy; and no doubt this is true as a general principle; but it is better to see boys and young men politically wrong on this point, than prematurely wise, and hard-hearted, and selfish. There were no crumbs thrown to the poor Lazaruses at the shop door by the senior youths, who passed out from their feasting with-

out a look of sympathy or deed of charity for others.
But there was one exception: the youngest of the
boys, whose heart had not yet been seared by the red-
hot iron of worldly wisdom, whose natural feeling and
generosity flowed forth, slipped back into the shop,
and bought two large buns, which he unobservedly gave
to the poor children. The others on any day would
have preferred to spend their money in cakes, fruits,
liqueurs, cigars, and kid gloves; all of which, except
the gloves, are more or less injurious to the stomach;
and sensual, selfish indulgence is hateful when it is
unaccompanied by practical consideration for the real
wants of others.

Here is Mr. Ferguson's sketch of a greedy flea—a
fancy sketch of course; but greedy lads and greedy
fleas are nasty things to look at.

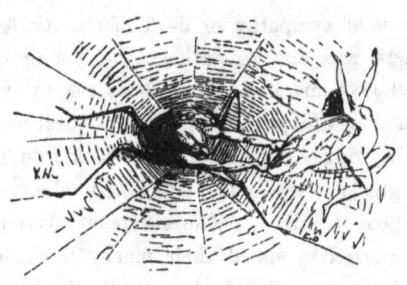

ZEKY NAASHON,
THE JEW OF PORTSMOUTH.

AN OLD MAN-OF-WAR'S MAN'S YARN.

DID you ever hear tell of Zeky Naashon, young gen'man ?
as cunning an old Jew, he was, as ever sold slops, and
passed off pinchbeck watches as gold ones, on board a
man-o'-war in Portsmouth harbour ? But now I come
to think of it, I don't suppose you ever did, seeing as
how, if he had lived to count a hundred years, which
he didn't, he'd have been dead long before any on you
was born. At one time there wasn't many who ever
set foot on the Point, or Common Hard either, who
didn't know old Zeky ; but let me see, that was when
I was a younker, and most of the gay fellows I knew
then have slipped their cables one after t'other for a
wider berth than we've got in this world. Ay, young
gen'man, them *was* times to live in, when plenty of the

shiners was to be had for a little fighting, and there
was plenty of ways to spend them; but now it's hard
work to get an honest penny any way. I'd like to see
them times over again, that I would; but it's no use
wishing for them, they are gone, and will no more come
back than a thirty-two pound shot would float up from
the bottom of the Atlantic. But I'm all adrift.
Then you never heard tell of old Zeky, sir?

Now I mind, sir, it's not probable that you should,
for the reasons I have said. Well, sir, there wasn't
such a Jew in all Portsmouth—and there were not a
few on 'em there—for turning a penny. There wasn't
a thing in the universal world Zeky hadn't got to sell,
always except a little honesty, and for the matter o'
that, he'd have had hard work to find it among his
commodities; and there wasn't many things he wouldn't
buy, at his own price, except the honesty I spoke of,
because you know that isn't to be bought; if it was,
why he'd have given just nothing for it, because as how
he didn't know its value. No sooner did a ship from
a foreign station drop her anchor at Spithead, and
shore-boats was allowed to come alongside, than Zeky
was to be found with his wares spread out between
two guns on the main deck, driving a brisk trade with
all on board. He'd got everything among his goods
from a sou'-wester to a shoe-tie for the men, and from
a ear-ring to a petticoat for the gals. Lord, he'd rig
Moll out with new gear from truck to kelson in no
time, and many's the dirty-looking drab has come on

board not fit to be seen, and gone on shore again as
fine as a princess in her holiday suit;—Jack, you see,
sir, paid for all. Zeky, why he took the cast-offs in
exchange. He'd got no end of slops—hats and shoes,
and jackets and trousers, and handkerchiefs of all
sorts and colours. Then he'd watches, and buckles,
and ear-rings (for in them days most seamen wore
them, as well as pigtails, and love-locks, and more's
the pity, to my thinking, that they've almost gone out
of fashion—that's to say of the matter of pigtails—one
does see ear-rings and love-locks now and then, and I
like the look on 'em—they reminds me of old days).
Then, as I said afore, he'd rings and seals, and baccy-
boxes, and scissors, and needles, and thread, and
knives without end, and brooches, and women's ear-
rings, and bonnets, and all sorts of female gear, of
which in my life I never could remember the names
rightly, except such as belongs to a ship;—by the
same token, you knows we are fond of rigging our
sweethearts and ships much in the same way, and
taking as good care of them. I likes to see them with
bonnets on, stays well set up, and canvas spread on
both sides, walking along at ten knots an hour before
a spanking nor'-easter.

But as I was saying about Zeky, he'd buy anything
the men brought home; and rum things some on 'em
were; and then he'd take all their old clothes off their
hands, and, more than likely, sell them again to the
same men as bran new. Then he was always accom-

modating to lend the officers, and men for that matter,
as much money as they wanted, provided they gave
him what he called security, which, to my eye, seemed
only slips of paper, but, somehow or another, he always
contrived to squeeze their pockets pretty dry before
he'd have done with them. Now I don't say, on any
manner of account, that all Jews are like Zeky, for
I've known several very decent, Christian-like chaps
among 'em, so I means nothing disrespectful to any
on 'em; but you know, sir, there are rogues among
all nations; for if there wasn't, one wouldn't be able
to tell who was honest. Howsomedever, with respect
to Zeky, if there ever was a big rogue, he was one to
a sartainty. He did look like one, too, or I don't
know who does; though nobody had a softer tongue,
nor more 'sinivating manners than he. He had been
many years in trade, and had now grown old; so he
was rather bent in his figure, and wore a long white
beard, or rather it weren't white, but a yellowish
dirty-brown colour. His nose was a rummish-look-
ing ornament, stuck on to the middle of his face, for
all the world like a hawk's beak, with a twinkling eye
on each side of it, which looked so black and piercing,
that one couldn't help thinking that he'd filched them
from the same bird, or mayhap swopped 'em for a
consideration of some sort or another. I don't know
where he got his teeth from, except out of the jaws of
a mangy cat, for I never saw any flying thing with 'em,
except it were a bat, to which his mouth weren't

P

altogether unlike. You may suppose, sir, he wasn't
considered much of a beauty; yet, though he was
known to be as big a rogue as ever breathed, he contrived to have dealings with everybody, and everybody
courted his favour, though he spit upon them, and
they hated him; but the truth is, they were afraid
on him, and he was rich. Many's the man who treats
the world, and the world treats, like old Zeky Naashon.

Now comes the wonderful part of my story. All
on a sudden Zeky disappeared, and no one knew what
had become of him. His house was shut up and his
stock-in-trade sold off, all except a few old shoes and
some cracked pitchers which no one would give nothing for at no price. He'd got in all his debts, but
I'm not quite so sure he'd paid all he owed, so people
never expected to see old Zeky back at Portsmouth
again. Why he went was equally a mystery. Some
people whispered one thing, some another; some said
he'd been discovered defrauding the revenue, which is
more than likely, seeing he'd been doing it all his life ;
others said he'd been making false money, or forging,
or robbing some one agin the law, or, at all events,
lighting a fire for Old Nick, which had made the
country too hot to hold him. Yet all the world knows
that he never came back again. There was no lack of
Jews in Portsmouth to carry on his trade, though I
doubt if there was ever a more cunning rogue escaped
the gallows than old Zeky, for the simple reasou be

cause he weren't born to be hung. What he was born to I'm going to tell you.

I had almost forgotten all about old Zeky, for you see, sir, I was a mere slip of a lad when he lived, when a circumstance happened which brought him back to my recollection. It was about seven or eight years afterwards, I mind: I had not long come home from sea, and was stopping with my old father, who lived in those days on the coast of Dorsetshire, not far from Corfe Castle. He didn't think there was any harm in doing a bit of free-trade now and then hisself, and as for me, it never came across my mind that there was any harm whatsomever in it. So it happened,—there's no use denying it, it was towards the end of November, when the days were getting very short and dark, and the weather very wild,—that notice was given to us that a crop was to be run, and our assistance asked to get the goods on shore. Of course, we couldn't refuse, and to make short of it, most of our men were engaged on the beach, when down came a troop of dragoons upon them, and a party of custom-house officers, which weren't like the revenue men of these days, mostly regular built seamen and honest fellows. Our people showed fight, and several on 'em was hurt, but at last they were obliged to cut their sticks, and run for their lives. My father and two of my brothers and I had been up to hide away some of the things at a place not far from our cottage, and were just returning when we heard the firing, and soon afterwards met two or three fellows running as hard as their legs would carry them away from the soldiers. We was thinking of getting back to our own cottage, and stowing ourselves away in bed, but we agreed we'd go a little further to see what was going on. We had got close down to the beach when father stumbled over something, and came right down on his face. We heard a deep groan when he fell, and thought it was him who uttered it, but when we picked him up again, we found he wasn't hurt, and that the sound proceeded from some one lying wounded on the ground. When we came to examine what was the matter with the stranger, we discovered that blood was gushing forth from a deep wound in his side, soaking right through his Guernsey frock and thick Flushing jacket; so we agreed that if he wasn't quickly attended to he would be dead, and as our cottage was the nearest, we had better take him there. We accordingly carried him up at once, and laid him on father's bed, and then, getting at the wound, we bound it up as well as we could to stanch the blood. He had got an ugly blow on his head which had stunned him, but he soon recovered his senses, and when he heard that we were going to send for the doctor he wouldn't let us, saying that it was of no manner of use, for that he'd got his sailing orders, and should be slipping his cable before he could possibly arrive. He was a stout, strong-looking man, somewhere about forty or fifty years old, and had on a thick suit of Flushing, with high boots to keep out the cold and damp. He was now pale as death, but his voice, though rather husky, was as strong as most men's. He and father knowed each other, it seems, and father afterwards said he had always been a wildish sort of a chap, but not so bad as he made himself out. He had belonged to the lugger which run the crop, but having landed, met his fate from the pistol of one of the dragoons. You'll be axing what all this has to do with old Zeky; now I'll tell you, sir.

When we was going to fetch the doctor, "Don't go," says he, "it's no manner of use; neither he, nor any man, can caulk my seams fast enough to keep me afloat, but if there was a parson within hail, I've got something on my mind which I should like to get clear off before I slips."

Now it happened that there wasn't a parson within ten mile of us, and, in those days, the chances were that he wouldn't be at home if we sent. So father told him, and axed him if he wouldn't do as well.

"I can't say as how you are much like a parson, Sleet," he answered; "but seeing we've been shipmates together, and always good friends, I'd rather unburden my mind to you nor to any one else, and mayhap what I say may not be thrown away on your youngsters there. It was just such a night as this seven years ago, all but one day, I was sitting in my cottage making a lobster pot, while my wife was in a low chair opposite to me mending my Guernsey frock before the fire, and my three children were just put to bed, when

I heard several taps at the door. I lived then, as you know, Jim, at Hamble. You remember the cottage close down to the river. I had then, with five others, a share in a cutter of thirty tons, called the *Pout*, in which we used to go over to Guernsey for lobsters, and do any other odd jobs which came in our way, we were no ways particular."

As you've often heard, sir, the Hamble men never had the best of names, and heaven knows they don't deserve more than they've got. I can scarcely tell why, but so it was, if there was any mischief any-where, a Hamble man was sure to have a finger in it. Their craft, too, were fast vessels, and were not only engaged in smuggling, but in the war time were as well known in the French harbours as mounseer's own Chassé Marées, for they used to carry out information to Jean Crapeau of all that was going forward at home, and got well paid for it you may be sure.

"Well, we was to sail the next morning with the first of the ebb, for Guernsey, and I was just thinking of turning in to be up betimes, when I heard the knock-ing at my door. 'Who's there?' I asked, taking a hanger which hung over the fireplace in my hand, for in those days it wasn't quite safe in a lone place to open one's door at night to a stranger. 'Who's there?' I sung out.

"'Let me in, my friendsh; God of Abrahamsh, I shall die of cold and wet if you keep me standing out longer in the rain,' answered a voice from without.

"'What's your name, my friend?' I asked in return, though I thought I knew the voice.

"'Zeky Naashon,' answered the voice without; 'have pity upon a poor old Jew.'

"'Ho, ho,' I thought, 'is it you, my jewel?' for I'd had a few little dealings with him not long before, and hadn't many doubts but that he had cheated me, though I couldn't bring it home to him; so I opened the door and let him enter. In he came all dripping with wet, and tottering under the weight of a large box he carried on his back, such as hawkers keep their spices in. It was so heavy, I know, that I wonder he could have carried it so many miles as he had done, all the way over from Portsmouth.

"'Well, Zeky, what is it you want with me?' I asked, after he had hung his outer coat before the fire to dry, and set down to rest himself.

"'Oh, God of Abrahamsh, I am a poor old Jew, and ruined, quite ruined,' he began.

"'I am sorry to hear it, Zeky,' I answered, though I didn't believe him.

"'It's a sad thing, a sad thing for a poor old man like me, but I'll tell you what I want to do. I want to get over to Rotterdam or Antwerp, or one of those places by to-morrow, or next day, and will pay you out of my small means if you will carry me there in your cutter.'

"I told him that I'd no objection, and I didn't suppose the rest of us would, if he'd make it worth our

while. He offered two pounds at first, but I told him
he'd have to wait long enough in England before he
got anybody to carry him where he wanted to go under
ten, and at last he agreed to give that sum. He
wouldn't turn in all night, I remember, but sat up
before the fire warming himself with his feet on his
box, for he wouldn't let it out of his sight for a
moment. Do you know, Jim, I've often seen him
sitting in the same place night after night, though I
know'd perfectly well he wasn't there. Yet it was just
like reality; there he would be with his feet on his
box, and his chin almost bent down to his knees, his
long beard and white hair streaming with wet, and the
palms of his hands turned up to warm at the fire, his
twinkling eyes shining all the time, just for all the
world like two hot coals. But I'm getting ahead of
my story. Well, I couldn't go to sleep, myself, all
night for thinking what a pity it was I hadn't made old
Zeky pay more for his passage, as I knew to a certainty that he had been after some roguery or other,
and would rather have given twice the sum than remain on shore, and perhaps have been sent to prison
or been hung. However, a bargain's a bargain, so
next morning we was up before daylight and aboard.
I told the rest what I'd done, and they of course agreed
to take the Jew wherever he wanted to go, though
they grumbled at my not having asked more for his
passage.

"It was scarcely light when we got under weigh

and beat out of Hamble Creek, with the wind at sou'-west, blowing rather fresh, and the weather thick and dirty. The Jew had stowed himself away below as soon as he got on board, and there he sat, just as he had done at my cottage, before the fireplace in the little cabin, moaning and groaning, and talking of his poverty. When we got off Calshot Castle, he popped his head up the companion hatch, just to see how we were getting on; but when we told him, just for a joke, that there was some one looking at him with a spy-glass from the top of the castle, down he dived again in no end of a hurry, trembling all over like a jelly-fish, and his teeth chattering as if they would jump down his throat. Seeing this, we all felt certain that he knew the beaks were after him, and that he was afraid of being nabbed for something or other he had done. He was in such a fright that he didn't venture to show again till, after running out at St. Helen's, we were a good two miles clear of the Wight. He then came on deck again, either because he found it close below, or didn't like his own company; and now, thinking him-self safe, his spirits rose so much that he began to joke and chuckle in his own peculiar way.

" 'Ha, ha, my shons, you have a verish pretty craft, verish pretty. She would run away from a king's cutter like lightning. Ha, ha!'

" 'Ay, ay, Zeky; faster nor that too, if we had tubs or silks on board, or anything of value,' I answered; 'but now, of course, if one was to chase us, we'd let

her overhaul us directly, and mayhap she wouldn't take
the same trouble again when we had really got something on board. You understand that, Zeky, don't you?'

"On hearing this, he was in a great taking, and
swore we shouldn't get anything from him if any
cutter came near us. As luck would have it, not ten
minutes after he had said this, the mist cleared away
a little to the west'ard, and we made out a large
cutter at the back of the island, standing to the
east'ard. We soon saw that she was the *Scout*, one of
the fastest cruisers, as you remember, on the station.
We, however, had nothing else to do but to stand
steadily on, for if we had shown signs of flight, she,
of course, would have been after us. The Jew took
it very diffcrently to us, and I never saw a poor
wretch in such a fright, for he made sure the cutter
was sent to look after him. To us it mattered nothing,
for even if the cutter had boarded us, she could do
nothing with us, and as for the Jew, none of us
supposed that her people would have taken any notice of him; so leaving one man at the helm, and
another to keep a look-out ahead, while Zeky was
holding on to the weather-bulwarks, with his eye to
windward to watch what the king's cutter was about,
the other four of us went below to smoke a pipe, and
to take a drop of something to drink. While we was
sitting round the fire, for it was bitterly cold for the
time of year, as the devil would have it, our eyes fell
on the Jew's strong box.

" ' I wonder if that ere box is full of gold,' said Joe Hudson, our skipper, blowing a cloud of smoke round his face, to hide the expression which he felt was in his countenance.

" The words he spoke were simple enough, but somehow or other there was something in the tones of his voice which made us all know what was passing in his mind. We looked just down on the deck of the cabin; then our eyes met, but no one for some time dared to speak a word.

" ' It seems very heavy,' said Joe, wanting to get an answer from some of us.

" ' Maybe it is,' said Bill Davis. ' I didn't lift it.'

" Those words were enough to break the spell.

" ' I never felt a box so heavy, for its size,' says I, to Joe Hudson.

" ' The Jew seems to set great store on it,' he answered.

" ' He sat up, and watched it all last night,' says I.

" ' I wonder what he intends to do with so much gold,' says Bill. ' if it is gold.'

" ' Oh, he'll go and settle down in Germany, and turn gentleman, after cheating honest Englishmen all his life,' says Joe.

" ' The box must hold some thousand pounds,' says I.

" ' Yes, it's very heavy,' observes Joe, quietly.

" ' It's a pity,' says Davis.

" ' What's a pity?' I axes.

" 'That a Jew should be so rich,' says he, quickly.

" 'It is,' says Hudson.

" 'There are many rich rogues,' says I.

" 'There are,' says Joe.

" 'Come,' sung out Tom Hawker, who was always a wild dare-devil chap, 'why are you shilly-shallying, and backing and filling that way? Why can't you speak out, like men, and say what you do mean? Why can't you say you want the Jew's money?—it'll come to that.'

" 'But no one said we wanted the Jew's money, said Hudson, repeating his words.

" ' *Said!*—no one *said*—but we *thought* it,' says Tom. 'Why should we be afraid to speak out?'

" 'Hush! hush!' says Joe, 'the Jew will hear you.'

" 'What am I to be afraid of the Jew for?' axes Tom, with some briskness; 'he's more cause to be afraid of *us*. No one *said* we wanted his money—but we all *do* want it.'

" 'How are we to get it?' axes Hudson, coming to the point.

" 'Run down channel, and land him on the coast of Cornwall,' says I: 'he'll be afraid of coming back Portsmouth way to look for his money.'

" 'Not he,' says Hudson; 'he'd venture into —— to get it; and depend upon it, if we land him in England, we shall be blown upon.'

" 'Then put him on shore in France,' says Davis. 'he won't give us much trouble there.'

" 'You don't know how a Jew loves his money, Bill, or you wouldn't say that,' says Joe. 'Why, he'd follow us from one end of the world to the other to look for it, while he'd got a leg to walk with.'

"Then land him in the middle of the channel," says Tom; 'he'll not come back from there to trouble us, I'll warrant.'

" ' What do you mean?' axes Hudson, all in a fluster, though it *was* what *he hisself* had been thinking on.

"What do I mean? why, that dead men tells no tales,' answers Tom, boldly; 'that's what I mean. I likes to speak out, instead of tacking about in the way you three have been doing.'

"Why, that would be murder,' says Davis, with his teeth going; for he was a timid man, though not a bit better nor the rest on us : he was afraid of being a villain.

" ' Murder be hanged,' says Tom; 'it would only be the murder of a Jew; and who is to know anything about it if we keep a quiet tongue in our heads?'

" ' What will Jim and Sam say to it?' axes I. 'We han't consulted them.'

" ' There's no need of axing them,' says Hudson; ' we may do it as if it was done by chance, and no one be a bit the wiser for it.'

" ' How?' says Tom Hawker, tipping the wink to me, for he knowed all along what Hudson was driving at, for he was a precious old villain, there's no denying it.

"I'll show you,' says Hudson, 'when the time comes, if we are all agreed.'

"'I am,' says Tom, 'if the d——l take me for it.'

"'And I,' says I.

"'And I,' says Davis, 'only I hope we shan't be found out.'

"'Well, then,' says Hudson, 'the matter's settled.'

"We didn't say another word, but went on deck directly.   There was the Jew, holding on by the weather-bulwarks, and looking with all his eyes at the cutter, which came bowling along after us; but as our craft was a fast one, she didn't gain much on us.

"'Oh, mein Gosh! mein Gosh!' sung out old Zeky, 'that cutter will overtake us.   Mein good captainsh, can't you clap on more sail, and get away from her?'

"'That would only make her think there was something wrong,' answered Hudson; 'we'd much better take in two reefs in our mainsail, and haul down the foresail, and she'll soon pass us.   To my mind, she's only standing the same course we are, and perhaps is after one of those sail ahead.'

"'If dat is sho, if de offisher should come on board, I will turn in and pretend to be a shick man,' says Zeky, who rather liked the thought of playing a trick in any way.

"'Down with you, then,' says Hudson, 'and we will let you know when the cutter has passed us.'

"Accordingly, Zeky dived down below, and turned

into one of our berths, where we covered him up all but his head with a blanket. There he lay, his sharp eyes twinkling away like two sparks of fire, and his teeth chattering through cold and fright. As it was coming on to blow pretty fresh, and the sea was getting up, we had a good excuse for shortening sail, and the cutter, which wasn't thinking all the time a bit about us, soon passed ahead. When we told this to Zeky, he turned out of his berth, and after taking a look at his money-box, he came on deck again, rubbing his hands at the thought of being safe. He little knew what was in store for him. The wind had been shifting about for some time, and now settled down in the nor'-west, blowing big guns; the black heavy seas came rolling along after us, topped with white foaming heads. At the same time it came on again thick and dirty, and there wasn't anywhere another sail to be seen.

" 'This will do for us," says Hudson, walking for'ard with Hawker, so as to be out of ear-shot of the Jew. 'Do you, Tom,' says he, 'take the helm, and we'll tell Sam and Jim to go below; then we'll get the Jew to sit up on the companion, and if the sail jibes and the boom knocks him overboard, it's no fault of ours.'

" 'I understand ye,' answered Tom, 'but for my part, if I had the management, I'd, without more ado, heave him neck and heels into the sea. There's no choating the devil, you know.'

"No sooner had Sam and Jim gone below, than Joe Hudson ranges up alongside Zeky, and says he,—

"'You'll be more comfortable, and out of the way, Zeky, if you sits up there on the companion-hatch.'

"Zeky didn't much like moving, but when we told him that if a sea came on board he'd be safer there, up he got, staying himself up with both his arms. We was now, you knows, running right afore the wind, with two reefs down in the mainsail, tumbling about like a drunken duck. Tom was at the helm. Hudson, Davis, and I, went for'ard. There sat the Jew, little thinking that his hour had come.

"'Will it do?' sung out Tom. 'Will it do?'

"'Mind your helm!' says Hudson.

"Tom knew what that meant. Over came the heavy boom—crash—it struck the old Jew right amidships, and carried him away like a feather into the boiling sea. He gave one loud, dreadful shriek. I never heard anything like it, and often's the time it has rung in my ears since in many a heavy gale, till I've thought I saw the old man perishing before my eyes. Sam and Jim rushed on deck.

"'What's that?' says they, frightened to death.

"'The Jew overboard!' sung out Hudson.

"'Oh, mein Gosh, mein Gosh! shave me!' cried the Jew, for a wide gown he had on kept him floating high out of the water; and if ever I saw a horrid face, it was his.

"'Swim on board!' answers Tom, laughing.

"The cutter shot by him, and there he was, bobbing about, his head and arms just out of water, shrieking for help among the tumbling, foaming waves.

"'He's a-following the vessel, and is going to haunt us for ever!' sung out Davis, in a dreadful fright.

"And sure enough, as we looked, there was the Jew following in our wake, with a mass of foam bubbling and hissing round him. Even Joe Hudson didn't like the look of it, and Jim and Sam were ready to die with fright.

"'Oh, take me on board! take me on board, kind men, and you shall have von half of all de little monish I have got at home!' cried Zeky, as loud as the salt water would let him.

"'Thank you for nothing, Mr. Naashon,' answered Tom Hawker, jeering at him.

"'Ay, ay, we'll haul you on board! What are you staring at?' he says, looking at Davis.

"'Don't you see the Jew's got hold of a warp which that lubber, Sam Jones, left towing overboard.'

"So it was; and it was wondersome how fast the Jew held on. He didn't like to part with his gold.

"'You shall have all my monish; all, all, all!' sung out Zeky, in his agony.

"'Haul him on board,' says Hudson, giving a look at Tom, while he took the helm.

"Tom understood him, and slackened the warp

Q

several fathoms. The old man felt the strain taken off his arms, and didn't grip hold as fast as before.

" 'Now haul away, and get the Jew on board!' cries Tom.

"We hauled away. Suddenly the rope tautened again; the strain was more than he could resist. With a loud shriek, he let go. As he dropped astern, he threw up his arms grasping at nothing, and when he found that there was no chance for him, he turned to and cursed every mother's son of us in his own tongue; the sound of his screeching voice ringing in our ears, till the waves washed over him, and he sank for ever. Oh, those curses didn't go for nothing, as you shall hear. They were fearsome things. None of us spoke for some time, for the murder was on the conscience of all. Tom Hawker braved it the best. 'Well,' says he, after we'd run on some way, 'since the Jew's overboard, and we are his heirs, we may as well see what he's left us in his strong box. He said he'd give us it all if we'd haul him on board. We did haul, only he chose to let go, which was no fault of ours, you know.'

"On this we all laughed, and heaving the cutter to, went down below, all six of us, to open his box. We weren't long in knocking the cover off, when, instead of finding a box full of gold, the greater part of it was in crowns and shillings, and all sorts of ornaments and precious stones, which weren't of much use to us, as we didn't know their value. Then there was whole handfuls of copper, which he hadn't time to get changed, I suspect, but not more than eighty sovereigns in gold, though there was several strips of paper which Hudson said was bills of exchange; but we were afraid of doing anything with them, so we tore them up and threw them overboard. After all, we didn't get fifty pounds apiece, and for this we had sold our souls to the devil. Little good came of it, you may be sure, for the money was soon gone, and nothing remained but the thoughts of the cursed deed. Well, when we'd divided the money, and cut the box up and burnt it, we shaped a course for Guernsey. We there took in the cargo of lobsters we first intended to go for, and returned to Hamble.

"When we got home we couldn't bear the look of each other's faces, for, in truth, I believe we was afraid of one another, so we sold the cutter, and all went different ways. Now it's a fact not one of us six will have died a natural death. Tom Hawker went out to the West Indies, and I heard, not two years after, that he was hung as a pirate, at Port Royal, in Jamaica. Joe Hudson got triced up too, about the same time, on the Isle of Dogs, for shooting a revenue-officer. Sam and Jim Jones was both run down in a fishing-boat at sea, and never heard of more. Davis was pressed on board a man-o'-war, and fell overboard in a gale of wind, when no boat could be lowered to pick him up, and here am I, the last of the six, just slipping my cable with a pistol-shot in my side.

"There, Jim, I've unburdened my mind to you, and I hopes your youngsters will take warning from my fate."

The dying man held on till morning, groaning with pain, and sometimes raving about the Jew, whom he declared he saw sitting before the fire warming his hands and turning round his burning eyes towards him.

Just as the first faint streaks of light appeared in the sky, he sat bolt upright in bed, with his arms stretched out, and sang out, "Haul away, haul away ye devils, or I can't hold on any longer." Then suddenly he fell back, the rattle was heard in his throat, and he was dead. He evidently thought himself the drowning Jew.

There, young gen'man, that's the way how I knowed for a sartainty what became of Zeky Naashon, the Jew of Portsmouth.

Delighted at being free from all care, and with no burden to carry,
Jack sprang up, esteeming himself the happiest boy alive. *Page 237.*

HAPPY JACK.

A STORY TO TELL TO YOUNG BROTHERS AND SISTERS AT CHRISTMAS.

ONCE upon a time there lived a peasant boy, named Jack. He had served his master honestly and faithfully for several years, during which time he had never seen his poor old mother, who lived many miles distant. At last Jack began to feel homesick, and asked his master to pay him his wages, and allow him to return home.

His master gave him a lump of gold as large as Jack's head; and it was, I can assure you, none of the smallest. Very well satisfied, Jack packed his heavy burden in a cloth, and set out on his journey. He proceeded very merrily for some time, whistling and singing, for he thought how pleased his mother would be to see him bring home such a lump of gold. At last he began to feel tired—for carry it as he would, on his head or across his shoulder, the gold was very heavy,—so he sat down to rest himself on a stone by the wayside, and in a few minutes a man passed by riding on a beautiful horse. "Oh!" exclaimed Jack, "riding is a noble exercise; I wish I had a horse."

The horseman stopped when he heard Jack's speech,

and asked him what he had in his bundle, it appeared so very heavy?

"It is gold, pure gold," replied the boy, "and I cannot carry it any further." So saying, he threw it down on the ground.

"If you would really like to have the horse, I don't care if I give it to you in exchange for that great load," said the man.

Jack jumped up quite delighted with the proposal. "Take it," he exclaimed, "it is a bargain. I shall never walk on my own legs again, when I have a horse to carry me."

The man thinking that the foolish boy would soon repent of his bargain, picked up the gold and ran off as fast as possible.

Jack, who had never been on a horse in his life, with some difficulty clambered into the saddle, and galloped on towards his native village. But not long could the poor fellow keep his seat; the horse suddenly stumbling over a stone, Jack was thrown over its head, and fell heavily to the ground like a sack of oats. He was completely stunned, and unable to move for some time.

A peasant, who was passing by leading a cow to market, caught the horse, and brought it to where Jack lay prostrate. He assisted him to rise; and Jack, looking very sheepish, said: "No more riding for me it does not agree with my constitution. You are a happy man, my friend, to possess such a nice quiet cow; you may drink milk every day, and have good butter and cheese, and never need to run the risk of being thrown down and nearly killed, as I have just been, by that furious horse of mine."

"Oh," replied the cunning peasant, "if my cow pleases you so much, I will give it to you in exchange for your horse, which certainly seems to be a spirited animal, and rather hard to manage."

"A good riddance," said Jack, "and I consider myself most lucky to make such a bargain." He accordingly drove the cow on, whilst the peasant mounted the horse, and disappeared in a moment.

When Jack arrived at the little inn where he intended to dine, he ordered a good dinner and spent every farthing he had; for he thought that, having a cow, he was no longer in need of money. He then again set off towards his native village; but after some time he felt thirsty, and thought he would like to have a draught of milk. "How fortunate I am to have such a fine cow," said he to himself; and thereupon he attempted to milk her, but so clumsily, that he could not obtain a drop of milk; and the cow gave him such a kick in the face, that for several minutes he lay motionless on the ground. Just as he was recovering a little, a butcher passed by, driving a fine fat pig; he asked Jack what was the matter, and offered him some refreshment from a small flask he had in his pocket. Jack, having drunk a little, felt better, and related his adventures to his compassionate acquaintance. The butcher said that the cow was too old to give milk; she was only fit to be killed.

"Hem," said Jack, "I don't think an old cow will prove particularly tender to eat. Now a nice fat pig like that would give me some capital bacon and savoury sausages."

"My good friend," replied the butcher, "you may have my pig, and I will take the old cow; will that please you?"

"I shall be heartily glad to lose her," said Jack, inwardly rejoicing at his good luck. He then continued his journey, again merrily whistling, and thought to himself, "What a fortunate fellow I am; my losses are always richly repaired! How nice this fat little pig will taste! I quite long to have a bit of him." Shortly after a boy overtook him, carrying a goose under his arm. As they were going in the same direction, they entered into conversation, and the boy told Jack that the goose was intended as a present from his master to his son, whose child was going to be christened that day; "and," he continued, "it will be the daintiest dish that ever was seen; such another goose is not to be found in the whole country!"

"I would rather have my pig," said Jack; "I shall have more than one good dinner from his fat sides when I get home."

"Where did you get it?" said the other.

Jack told him all his adventures, and the boy listened with attention. At last he said, "Listen: I can tell

you a secret. In the next village there was a pig
stolen from the mayor last night. The thief has accused you of committing the crime, and the constables
are now searching for you ; I think there is one hiding
behind that hedge. If he should find you, you will
be arrested ; and instead of being comfortably seated
at your mother's fireside to-night, you will be enjoying
all the comforts of a jail."

" Oh dear, oh dear !" said poor Jack, " what an
unfortunate creature I am ! What shall I do ? "

" Quick !" said the other, " do you give me the pig,
and take my goose. I know all the by-paths in the
neighbourhood, and can soon manage to get out of
sight."

No sooner said than done, and ere Jack had gone two
steps, the bad boy and pig were no longer to be seen.

Jack laughed heartily at having so well contrived to
rid himself of the unlucky pig, and carried the goose
in his arms for some distance, calculating how much he
might make by the feathers, and what a nice dinner
he would give his mother. He had now arrived at the
next village to his own native place ; and as he passed
through the street, he saw a travelling cutler sitting at
his machine, and singing loudly to the music of his
wheel.

> "There came a young cutler one day,
> He sharpened your scissors and knives ;
> He has since then been far, far away,
> And again asks your custom, good wives."

" Scissors to grind." Whirr-whirr-whirr.

Jack stood for some time staring at the cutler; he was quite astonished to see him so merry at his work. At last he said, "You seem to like your trade. I suppose it is profitable; do you earn much by it?"

"Oh yes, friend," rejoined the cutler, "I am always happy, I have always money in my pocket. Have you got nothing but that goose? Where did you get it?"

"I exchanged it for a pig!" said Jack.

"And the pig?"

"I gave a cow for it."

"And the cow?"

"I got it in exchange for a furious horse."

"And the horse?"

"I paid a large lump of solid gold for it."

"And where did you find the gold?"

"I received it as wages for seven years' service."

Whirr, whirr, whirr! "Scissors to grind, scissors to grind!—you want nothing but a stone like mine to make your fortune. I have one lying by me which I could spare. Will you give me your goose for it?"

"Willingly," said Jack, "if you really think I can make my fortune with it."

"Just try," replied the man; and giving Jack an old whetstone and a pebble, which he picked up on the road, he received the goose, and Jack departed quite happy. The sun shone brightly; and feeling very tired and warm, the boy sat down to rest beside a well. Oh, thought he, as he stooped down to drink, what a foolish lad I was to take those stones; they are nearly as heavy as the gold was. Just at that moment, as he was leaning over the well, the stones rolled into the water: splash, splash! and they were gone.

Delighted at being free from all care, and with no burden to carry, Jack sprang up, esteeming himself the happiest boy alive, and arrived in good spirits at his mother's cottage.

HAPPY DAYS OF PUPPYHOOD.

BY AN OLD DOG.

MANY years have passed (at least to me they seem many) since I first saw the light, in the cottage of Jock Weasel, the gamekeeper of Gullysporan, and beheld the kind eyes of my mother "Jeanie," watching the development of my puppyish powers.

Her interesting contemplation of me was, however, suddenly interrupted by a creature who to my sight appeared a giant. This was no other than Willy Weasel, the gamekeeper's son, a stout lad about ten years old (I heard his mother say so the next day, when she boxed his ears for being idle), who seized unceremoniously on my respected parent, and dandled her on his knee, singing "Jenny's bawbee," while she, not liking to be thus treated before her puppies' newly-opened eyes, looked steadily up in his face, breathing through her clenched teeth, and very much inclined to bite his nose off; but this she did *not* do. And thus I was first introduced to Willy Weasel. Besides my mother and Willy, I soon became aware of two soft warm balls like myself, lying on their backs, with their noses under each other, and these turned out to be my brother Tommy, and my sister Toozy. My brother was, I think, named after Tommy Weasel the baby, whose cradle rocked in a corner, to the great danger of our little round heads, when we began to run about, without knowing exactly where we were going. I am sure I do not know who Toozy was named after. I was never called anything but "Pupsy" at first, but was differently named afterwards, as I shall show. There had been more than three of us, I know, for I once heard Willy say to his sister, "Eh, Maggie, they're very bonny, but the drooned anes were just as weel faured!" How sad to think that if these "drooned anes" had lived, they might have enjoyed life as I have done, and passed many happy days in hunting rabbits and rats! But I must proceed to narrate my own experiences without lingering over such mournful retrospections.

My earliest days of puppyhood were passed in a small barrel, which was indeed our mother's own house, close to the door of the gamekeeper's cottage, from which I was occasionally abstracted by Willy to be shown to Maggie, and have my nose dabbed into a saucer of milk, saved from their porridge, a treat which I at first by no means relished, and generally showed my ingratitude by putting my feet into the saucer, or sitting down in and upsetting it; but I soon learned to know what was good for me, and never refused milk in any shape.

Our mammy was the best of mothers, though she did not spoil us with too much kindness, and now and then knocked us over with every sign of anger, if we attempted to presume on her good nature, or take liberties. On such occasions we were always very penitent, yelped, and nestled close up to her. And then she would take pity on us, nibble us all over, and make up for her little show of ill-temper by nursing us very kindly.

The first few months of my life passed over thus, without anything at all remarkable. By degrees I got the use of my legs, and an irritating sensation in my gums showed that my teeth were coming. Oh, happy days of innocence! How little interest I then took in

these small white teeth, which, however, soon drew
Willy Weasel's attention, for I remember the first time
I made him feel them, he exclaimed, "Ma conscience,
Maggie! the wee yane's bittit ma thoomb!" And
here I must remark, that it is my belief I only bit him
in fun, for, though those teeth of mine have been freely
(perhaps *too* freely) used on some of my fellow-creatures,
no one can accuse me of ever snapping at man, woman,
or child.

As our teeth became developed, we were seized with
a constant wish to use them, and lost no opportunity
of doing so; but we soon found that we could not
gratify our gnawing propensities without unpleasant
consequences; and many a thump we got for tearing
and chewing whatever we could lay teeth on. Even
to this day, I remember the dreadful whipping old
Jock gave me for having, harmlessly, as I thought,
gnawed a big hole in a tartan plaid, which he had just
presented to Mrs. Weasel. I really wonder now, when
I think of it, that he did not then and there violently
put an end to my young existence; but if people *will*
leave such things within our reach, what *can* they
expect?

I passed many happy days basking in the sunshine
at the mouth of our barrel-home, or tumbling about
amongst the hay inside with my brother and sister. Our
dear mother was never chained up, but, until we were
old enough to run with her, she often started off, and
left us for a while to whimper a little at first, and then

worry each other, till we were tired and went to sleep. One day she had left us thus to our own devices; sister Toozy was fast asleep, and my brother and I were fighting behind the barrel, when our mother appeared, carrying in her mouth a brown creature with a long tail, which I saw as I rushed delightedly up to kiss her, —and of course the unusual sight arrested my attention. My mother then deposited the creature on the ground and set her foot firmly on it. "Bairns," said she, "shak the rotten." The brown creature squeaked and struggled. Immediately a strange and angry feeling filled my heart, and I became possessed with a determined wish to seize the animal. I made several very gallant snaps at its head, and once indeed my teeth must have been within half an inch of it, when an unfortunate event occurred. Tommy jumped on my back. He had come up behind, hearing the scuffle, but without knowing what was the cause of it. Toozy had just awoke from a sound sleep, and was sitting up and staring at the rat in astonishment, while I was making snaps at its head, when suddenly, as I have already mentioned, Tommy came behind and jumped on my back. The immediate consequence of this thoughtless act was, that I sprawled over with my nose on the rat, who took the opportunity to bite me severely, and would not let go till my mother seized and shook him well, after which she handed his remains over to us, and we practised the art of shaking "a rotten" for some time under her directions.

It was about this time that another event occurred which produced on my mind a deep impression, and raised bitter feelings of animosity which time has not dispelled. I was basking in the sun near the cottage door, when suddenly the angry barking of my mother awoke me, and Willy Weasel ran close past me, shouting "Shak her," and clapping his hands towards a corner in the wall at the other end of the cottage. In a moment I ran after him, and perceiving a white creature in the corner, ran straight up to it without really knowing what I was about, so much was I confused with the suddenness of my awaking from sleep. Judge then of my astonishment when I found myself dreadfully scratched by this white creature, and knocked over by a blow of her paw. Need I say that this was a cat? Willy went into fits of laughter, I yelled, and my mother took the opportunity to seize the cat by the back and shake her well; but she was not strong enough to do more, and that feline *wretch* was soon up the wall and over the house. This was my first introduction to a cat, and ever since that day the whole tribe have been my bitter enemies. I cannot say that I have ever caused the death of one of them, but on every possible occasion I have attacked and chased them, and if I have had my face scratched by their claws once, I have had it a hundred times.

My course of life, soon after this event, was altered, and I one day found myself shut up in a basket, with some hay to lie on, and carried off on a journey which to *my* mind seemed endless! I was jolted slowly over many miles of road, slung at the back of a carrier's cart, where all my yelping was of no avail. I yelped myself hoarse, and the little boys who ran after the cart and hung on behind, poked their fingers into the basket, and laughed at me. I cried for my mother, I cried for my brother and sister, and I cried for Willy Weasel. It seemed to me that my heart was broken, and the world empty; but soon after, when the good-natured carrier dropped a bone into the basket, I thought that all was *not* lost, and that there might be good things in the world with which I was still un-acquainted. We went on till night, and I forgot my woes in sleep. I have a faint recollection of being taken from the cart and put on something else which moved more quickly, but I really did not mind what happened, for I slept soundly, with my nose close to the well-picked bone, dreaming of my barrel-home, with my mother, and Tommy, and Toozy in it. I was awoke by the voices of children, and found myself still in the basket, but the daylight was streaming through the breathing holes in its side, and two big eyes were also staring in at me. Being in good spirits at the time, having just awoke from a refreshing nap, I stag-gered towards the eyes through the hay, and made a jump at them when I got near enough. This produced a scream, which frightened me dreadfully, and sent me rolling over on my back in fear and trembling.

"Oh, Charley!" I heard a child's voice say, "zi

puppy bite my eye!" and then three other voices joined
in shouts of laughter, while I still lay on my back,
wondering what they would do to me when they got
me out. But I was soon lifted from my temporary
abode, and found myself the centre of an admiring
circle, consisting of one big boy, and one little one, and
two girls. I did not know their names for some days
afterwards, but I may at once mention that they were
Lizzy, Mary, Charley, and Bobby Henderson. They
evidently expected me to begin to play with them at
once, for they danced round me and ran backwards and
forwards, speaking in an encouraging manner; but I
got confused, and frightened, and was obliged to sit
down and consider what I should do, when unfortunately Bobby fell over me, hurting himself and me
too, *especially me!* Of course I yelped with pain,
and then the other children took me up, and nearly
smothered me with kindness. They afterwards gave me
some milk and bread, and we soon became friends, and
went out to play on the lawn in front of the house.
While running about with them, I suddenly heard
behind me the noise of a dog's feet, and before I had
time to turn round, I was knocked over, and sent
spinning head over heels several times. I did not
attempt to rise, but lay perfectly still on my back, with
my legs in the air, keeping the corner of one eye open,
and beheld standing over me a large black dog, very
handsome, and, I thought, fierce-looking! I lay quite
quiet, and he proceeded to make a minute examination

of me; after which, I gradually rose and crept round him in a most humble manner. All this happened in less time than I have taken to tell it, and the eldest boy, Charley, now interposed, and raising me in his arms, said—

"Niger! this is my puppy, and you are not to bully him, but must take great care of him while I am away at school; for he is, you see, a very small puppy, and you could eat him if you liked, but you must be kind to him."

Niger heard this with attention, but proceeded to make some jumps at me, while Charley held me above his head. I soon discovered, however, that he was only in fun, and from that day to this I have ever found in Niger a true and powerful friend, always ready to take my part; and although I fear I then often tried his temper greatly by biting him (*nominally* in fun) much harder than I would have liked myself, he never once lost his temper, or punished me as he might easily have done if he pleased.

Charley Henderson was now my master, and named me "Wasp," but he had to start for school in a few days, and then I was left in charge of his sisters and little brother, who would soon, I think, have spoilt me with kindness, had not my education been attended to by Mr. Mitchell, the butler. Besides which, a watchful eye was kept on me by Niger, who, though kind, was not the dog to allow me to lead an idle or inactive life. And so some months passed on very happily. I seldom

thought much of my mother, and brother, and sister;
but soon got to love my new home, and spent my
time in learning to sit up, and behave myself in all
respects as a gentleman's dog should do, enjoying a
romp with the children and Niger every now and
then.

At last Charley Henderson came back from school,
and I scarcely knew him at first, he had grown so much.
His voice too had changed, and he seemed so strong
and rough, I was quite afraid of him. One of the first
things he did was to lift me up by my tail " to see if I
was game!" Perhaps the experiment was not quite
satisfactory, for he repeated it much oftener than I at
all liked. He was so kind as to decide that I should
be educated for field-sports, of which he was very
fond; and I was invested with a beautiful collar,
which, though of course proud of, I found very inconvenient.

I must now tell you of my first rabbit-hunt, with
which I will conclude this brief memoir of my happy
days of puppyhood; for soon after that I had my
proper work assigned to me, and was treated as a
grown-up dog.

Soon after my master's return from school, in fact I
think the very first day, he took Niger and me out
with him in the early morning, and we started in the
direction of a wood not far from the house, where there
was a thick under-growth of bushes and ferns. Niger
seemed much excited at first, and I did not at all

understand the cause; but he knew where we were going, and showed his delight by shouting (in dog Latin, of course)—

"Rabbits! rabbits! rabbits! What fun! what fun! what fun! Rabbits! rabbits!"

When we reached the wood, Niger became quiet, and began snuffing about with his nose to the ground, in what I thought a very ridiculous manner; so I did my best to interrupt him in his occupation, and tried to bite his ears, but he suddenly started off at a great pace, with my master after him, leaving poor little me quite alone. I tried to keep up with them at first, but could not, so became terrified, and ran about yelping, without knowing what to do; but happening to put my nose to the ground, a delightful odour arrested my steps, and turned me in a new direction. Instinct told me that a rabbit had passed that way, and like a shot I was after him, as fast as my little legs would carry me! At first I was in a *whirl* of excitement, and quite unintentionally found myself calling out in our language—

"Here! here! here! Quick! quick! quick! Here! here! here!"

This I have afterwards discovered is called "giving tongue." I soon got out of breath, and as I had seen nothing, I was thinking of sitting down to rest, when suddenly Niger rushed past me, nearly upsetting me as the passed, saying—

"Well done, little un! keep your tail up!"

And soon after we came to a round hole in the ground,

under a bush, in which, from the charming fresh scent about it, there could be no doubt that rabbits lived. Niger stood panting over the hole, I lay down and gasped for breath, but as soon as I *could*, I got up, and being a very small dog, I went straight into the hole.

" Bravo! bravo!" snorted Niger, as he looked in after me, and gave a long sniff with his nose tightly shoved into the aperture, thereby nearly choking me; but I scrambled on, sometimes stopping a minute to widen the way in, by scratching where the hole was narrow. It was very dark, and I was beginning to wish myself safely out again, when my nose came against something soft and warm! Was it possible? Did my senses deceive me? Yes, they did! No, they didn't! A pause for an instant, and the next I was backing out of the hole, dragging after me *a rabbit*, which, with its legs stretched straight out, and sometimes kicking desperately, seemed very unwilling to leave his comfortable abode. A large rabbit would certainly have been too much for me, as I was so young, but fortunately this one was only half-grown, and I had the pride and satisfaction of getting him safely out. At the mouth of the hole I found Charley, as well as Niger, waiting for me, and they were both highly delighted when I brought the rabbit out. Charley said, " Shake it then, good dog!" but Niger saved me that trouble, for no sooner had I made my appearance than he seized the rabbit by the back, and though I hung on for a little, he swung me round so hard that I was obliged to let go, with nothing for my trouble but a mouthful of fur, which nearly choked me.

And now that I have tried to give you a sketch (I fear a very imperfect one) of some of my happy days of puppyhood, I must make my bow-wow, wag one tail, and bring the other to a conclusion.

SIR GANDO THE VALIANT.

A MERRIE TALE OF CHIVALRIE.

Timo the tailor sat busily at work. Swelling and ambitious dreams occupied his brain; for, though mean of birth and small of stature, great was that little tailor's bump of self-esteem, and doughty were the deeds which, in imagination, he achieved.

The day was sultry, and the tailor sorely troubled by swarms of flies, when, perceiving a number settled on a melon which lay near, he suddenly smote them with the garment he was making, and slew seven. "Oh, ho!" quoth the tailor, "now I am a hero! Seven at a stroke!" and, forthwith casting aside his needle, he accoutred himself in full armour, and, bearing on his shield in letters of gold the proud motto, "Seven at a stroke," he departed, to seek fortune and further glory in the world of chivalry.

It chanced one day that, as he lay asleep in a grassy dell, the king of the country through which he was journeying rode by, with many nobles and attendants, and all stopped to comment on the gallant and warlike guise of the unknown knight. The motto on his shield was read, and excited some anxiety, as it was evident he was a very undesirable foe, while, could his services be secured, he would be invaluable as a friend.

The little tailor awoke amid the eager discussion of the subject, and accepted the honourable salutations he unexpectedly received with calm and undaunted impudence. He was without delay introduced to the king in the character of a warrior seeking employment for his invincible sword, and was entertained at court with great honour.

With many regrets that, being at peace, he could for the present offer the brave stranger no active employment in his service, the king begged he would not refuse to take the command of a body of his troops, and reside at court in the enjoyment of wealth and luxury, till such time as fortune should open the way to further deeds of fame.

With a very good grace, the valiant tailor submitted to a life of inaction, and wore the laurels of imaginary glory with admirable dignity. But, ere long, many of the good king's officers and courtiers became jealous of the favoured stranger, and the monarch found that he should lose some of his best servants if he retained him at court. Yet he feared the resentment of so powerful a knight, should he dismiss him. After anxious deliberation, the king sent for Sir Gando Threadalbane (for such was the name he had assumed), and informed him that, as a mark of the high esteem in which he held his valour and prowess, he had selected him to go on an expedition requiring the greatest courage and personal strength, and the success of which was to be rewarded with nothing less than the hand of the princess royal in marriage, and half his kingdom. Now these promises dazzled Sir Gando amazingly, and he professed himself fit and ready to do anything in the world; nor did his confidence abate when the king explained that the work in hand was the positive death and destruction of two terrific giants, of cruel and cannibalish propensities, who inhabited a gloomy forest, and were the scourge and dread of the country. None hitherto sent against them had escaped a fearful fate, but the king hoped everything from his noble friend Sir Gando, and offered a strong body of troops to assist him.

It is certain the little hero had no wish at all to find himself in the larder, or smoking on the table of these

monsters, and equally certain that he had not the re-
motest idea how he was to avoid that remarkably un-
comfortable situation. Yet, trusting to fortune and
his wits (his sword he never dreamt of!), he maintained a dauntless bearing, and gaily set forth on his
perilous enterprise.

Arrived at the outskirts of the forest, and desiring
his attendants to await him there (they, be it known,
nothing loth to obey), Sir Gando made his way cautiously towards the deepest recesses of the dark and
silent woods.

The atmosphere was still. An oppressive gloom
overhung the place; but suddenly, as he advanced, he
heard an unearthly noise, and perceived the leaves and
boughs of one particular tree waving to and fro with a
strange, strong, regular motion, quite unaccountable,
until, as he crept nearer, he discovered asleep on the
ground beneath it the two gigantic and fearful beings of
whom he was in search. Their mighty snoring it was
which he heard, and which, with strong blasts, made
their leafy canopy bow. The sight made poor Timo
tremble and turn pale, and for a moment inclined to
flee; but remembering the reward, and summoning his
wits to the support of the knightly character of Sir
Gando, he filled his pockets with stones, and, hastily
scrambling up into the tree, placed himself on a branch
which overhung the giants. Then with the stones he
began to pelt one of them about the head. Very soon
the monster raised himself, and, glaring around for an

enemy in vain, he fiercely demanded of his companion
what he meant by daring to strike. He, of course,
denied the charge, and, after some high words, they
lay down.   No sooner did they snore again, than the
tailor betook himself to pelting the other, who, in his
turn, started up in a fury which was with difficulty
appeased by his friend.   Once more they composed
their gigantic limbs to rest, and closed their bloodshot
and fiery eyes; but the dexterous Sir Gando now contrived to drop heavy stones on each hideous head at the
same moment, when, with a fearful roar, both giants
sprang to their feet, and attacked each other in frantic
rage, tearing up trees and rocks, and hurling them at
each other with such dire effect that they both fell
dead, shaking the solid earth for a mile round with the
shock, and making the whole forest echo with their
dying howls.   During this awful combat, the poor
little hero's courage had been fast evaporating, especially as he every minute expected his tree to be up-
rooted for a club.   But joyfully assuring himself that
they were really no more, he slipped from his perch,
and, with his sword, inflicted many wounds, which
certainly would have been deadly, on their prostrate
bodies.

Then, rejoining his followers, he bade them ride into
the forest, if they had any curiosity to behold his slain
adversaries.

Nothing could exceed their amazement at his speedy
and complete victory; and they returned to the city to

report the marvellous news. Sir Gando appeared before
the king, expecting to receive the promised reward;
but the monarch, secretly regretting that the unknown
adventurer had survived to claim so dear a treasure as
his daughter, determined once more to attempt to dispose of the inconvenient hero, and with flattering
words requested him, as a particular favour, to exert
his prowess once more before his marriage, and rid the
country of a very large and dangerous unicorn, which,
roaming in an almost impenetrable forest, issued forth
continually, and did mortal hurt to the neighbouring
inhabitants. The amiable Sir Gando Threadalbane
kindly agreed to postpone his happiness, and give this
satisfaction to his future father-in-law; and, taking a
strong rope, he bade his attendants lead on to the
forest.

Arrived there, he, as before, chose to enter it alone;
and had not proceeded far when he beheld the unicorn
charging him full speed with levelled horn, that being
its mode of attack. Sir Gando was not anxious to
prove the sharpness of that terrible spear in his own
precious person; he stood still with his back to a tree
till the animal seemed close upon him, then, lightly
slipping aside, the horn of this fleetest and fiercest of
the equine race pierced to the very heart of the tree,
and remained immovably fixed. Now was the tailor
glad at heart; and, securing the creatures legs with the
rope without difficulty, as it seemed stunned by the
shock against the tree and despatching it with his

sword, he summoned his men, and, causing them to
extract the horn, cut off the singular head of the unicorn, and returned to present the trophy to his bride.
The king could not deny that Sir Gando had well and
fairly earned his reward; yet once more he sought to
escape the obligation to bestow it, by getting rid of the
lawful claimant.

"Noble and valiant Sir Gando," he exclaimed,
"you are a matchless and invincible knight. Your
deeds are brilliant, and surpass all I know. For my
own part, I am amply satisfied, and ready to fulfil the
conditions. Will you excuse a woman's whim, and
gratify the queen by slaying an enormous and savage
wild boar, which hitherto has been assailed not only in
vain, but to the destruction of all who have attempted
it? The lair of the monster is in a darkly-wooded and
rocky glen, close by the country palace I design for
your residence during your honeymoon, which accounts
for the queen's, and I may add, the dear Princess
Highbornia's anxiety to have it destroyed. Now, I
scarcely like to press the matter, the danger is so immi-
nent. It seems encroaching on your patience, but—"

"Say no more, your Majesty!" cried poor Timo,
irresistibly flattered, although really not over-pleased
at the prospect of more danger. "It shall not be said
I left anything undone for the safety or pleasure of the
fair Princess Highbornia."

Taking guides to conduct him to the haunts of this
dangerous and powerful wild beast, Sir Gando departed;

and, on reaching the place, advanced alone to the perilous encounter, for which he had not long to wait. The
savage boar no sooner saw the intruder, than, taking aim
with lowered head, he made at him full tilt with glaring
eyes and foaming mouth, his horrid tusks threatening
the most fearful death. This time the little tailor
thought it was all up with him; his heart beat fast,
his eyes grew dim; and, glancing round in vague hope
of an idea, he perceived an old ruined building, into
which, with the speed of despair, he rushed, with the
boar at his heels.

The single window of the little ruin was high. He
clambered up to it, sprang through it to the ground,
flew like lightning round the walls, and banged the
door close shut, thus imprisoning his furious foe. Then,
hastily returning to the window, he pierced the raging
boar with successive arrows from his bow, until it fell
exhausted from loss of blood, and soon expired.

Now the king dared not again run the risk of mortally
offending this brave knight, whose prowess was so well
tried, and whose fame was spread far and wide; so he
resolved to do the thing with a good grace, and celebrated the nuptials with prodigious splendour. The
Princess Highbornia being fortunately in love with no
one else, accepted her fate with all becoming submission
and aristocratic indifference.

A proud and happy man was little Timo; and some
time passed smoothly, when it began to be observed
that the princess occasionally looked anxious and per-

plexed; and at length, one morning, she desired
audience of the king and queen, and told them that her
husband said very strange things in his sleep, quite unaccountable, in fact, unless—she hesitated, and grew
pale—"unless he had been—a——"

"What, my daughter? Speak, dearest child!"

"——Been a—*murderer?*" suggested the queen.

"Pirate? spy? traitor?" cried the king.

"Ah no! worse, I think," replied the princess; and
she hid her face, and faintly whispered, "A tailor!"

The queen went into hysterics, and the king into a
passion on the spot; and it was some time before the
princess could explain that the expressions which led
her to this painful conclusion were such as these: "Boy,
bring me the goose;" "Sew on those buttons, and be
sharp about it;" "What! lost the needle again. I
shall crack that thick skull with the yard-measure some
day;" and many other shocking things to the like
effect.

The thought of his royal daughter having been
bestowed on a tailor was not to be tolerated with an
instant's calmness. A watch was set that night at the
door of the apartment, with strict orders that on the
utterance of any words to prove his base and plebeian
origin, the pretended knight should instantly be dragged
into the courtyard, and hung to the lamp-post. This
did really appear very hard lines to the poor fellow
when the plot was made known to him by a secret
friend; for he naturally thought that he had, one way

or another, very fairly won his spurs by this time, although he had certainly assumed them somewhat prematurely. He disliked the idea of a midnight execution uncommonly, and shuddered at the notion of being whisked out of his warm bed, and set swinging by the neck in the cold night air till he was dead. However, he made no attempts to escape, and retired to rest at the usual hour, soon appearing to be sound asleep.

The band of armed men came softly and cautiously to their station, and remained in eager watch for the words which were to be Timo's death-warrant.

Soon his voice was heard, in dull thick tones at first, as speaking in heavy sleep, " I must finish these trousers to-night. Where are the shears, boy? be quick, stupid!" Then, by degrees, more and more clearly, more and more rapidly, more and more loudly, came the words, "Must I hit you over the knuckles with the yard-measure? Beware how you anger me. Have not I slain seven at a stroke; slaughtered two giants; captured and put to death the greatest of unicorns; destroyed an unconquerable wild boar; and *now*," he thundered, springing out of bed with a clash of steel, "down with the cowardly knaves who stand behind the door!" The men tarried not to see it opened, but fled in dismay. And so the royal family were fain to hush the matter up, and put a good face upon it after all; while the prudent and forbearing, as well as valiant tailor, had the wisdom to avoid showing that he had been fully aware of their kind intentions on that memorable occasion. And thus, all parties tacitly consenting to let bygones be bygones, little Timo long flourished as the famous Sir Gando Threadalbane, and in process of time ascended the throne as King Consort.

THE FLOWER OF THE PRAIRIES.

It is well known that a good deal of superstition prevails among the aboriginal inhabitants of North and South America—the "Red Indians," as we call them. These "Red Men" are subdivided into numerous tribes, differing in many minor respects from each other, yet all bearing a general similitude. They have each their own laws, which almost everywhere are severe, energetic, and promptly administered. Each tribe has also its peculiar customs; but there are some features of Indian life common to all. Hospitality is a virtue highly esteemed among them all, and fortitude under suffering,

and wild valour in battle, are qualities as imperative in
the character of an Indian "Brave," or warrior, as
they used to be among the savage Berserkir of ancient
Scandinavia. Like the followers of Odin, also, the
Indians deem that personal courage and feats of arms
are the surest passports to happiness in a future world.
They all believe in the immortality of the soul, and
admit the existence of a Supreme Being. This Being
they call "The Great Spirit," or "Master of Life."
And their "medicine-men," who are at once physicians,
priests, and prophets, frequently pretend to have had
communication with this Great Spirit, either directly
or indirectly, through the medium of inferior deities,
a sort of household gods, images that are held in reverence among the people, or animals which are supposed,
among some tribes, to be ministering agents to "The
Great Spirit," or to the still more dreaded "Spirit of
Evil." In some parts of Florida *snakes* are supposed to
be endowed with this supernatural power. There is
much of fancy and poetical beauty in the mythology of
the Indians; they deem that every tree, every rock,
every breeze that agitates the air, every star that shines
in the heavens above, has a spirit; the Aurora Borealis
is a dancing spirit, the Milky Way is the path of spirits,
and here is a resemblance to the imagery of the Scan-
dinavian mythology, in which the rainbow is described
as the bridge over which disembodied spirits pass to
heaven. The Indians consider that storms and thunder
are manifestations of the wrath of the Great Spirit;

while success in war and in hunting are evidences of his favour. They have some undefined notion of the possibility of the spirits of the dead revisiting this material world, and though not, like some of the natives of Asia, holding as their creed the doctrine of the transmigration of souls, they yet think the spirits of the departed may occasionally assume the appearance of airy creatures belonging to our earth, such as birds or butterflies. But it is the happy spirits that take these pleasing forms. Less courteous to the poor birds is an Eastern superstition, which denominates certain birds on the Bosphorus, "Les âmes damnées." Flocks of these birds, which are not quite so large as pigeons, and have dark plumage, are sometimes seen passing up and down the Bosphorus with great rapidity. They are never observed to alight on land or water, they never deviate from their course or slacken their speed, and their flight is remarkably silent, for though so numerous and so close, the whirr of their wings is scarcely ever heard.

The American Indians have a deity whom they call "The Spirit of Sleep," a very useful invisible power, who employs multitudes of little sprites to close the eyes of weary mortals when they need repose. They have much faith in dreams, and that they believe in ghosts the following story may illustrate.

A tolerably large portion of the powerful Indian tribe of the Osages had been for some time encamped on the banks of a beautiful river, named the "Nick-a-

Nanse." Among them was a young hunter, the bravest and the handsomest of the chiefs belonging to the tribe. He was engaged to an Indian girl surnamed, on account of her extreme beauty, " *The Flower of the Prairies.*" The young hunter left her with her relations at the encampment, while he repaired to St. Louis to dispose of the products of the chase, and to buy some ornaments for her whom he loved so much.

After an absence of a few weeks he returned to the banks of the Nick-a-Nanse. But the camp had been raised, the tribe had quitted the place, and the foundations of the huts and the ashes of the extinct fires alone indicated the spot where his Indian brethren had dwelt when he left them.

At a little distance he observed, seated near the river, a woman who seemed to be weeping. It was the young girl to whom he was betrothed. He ran forward to embrace her, but she turned sadly away from him. The fear then took possession of his mind that some misfortune had happened to the encampment.

"Where are our people?" he asked, anxiously.

"They have removed to the banks of the Wagrushka."

"And what were you doing here quite alone?"

"I was waiting for you."

"Then let us hasten to join our people on the banks of the Wagrushka."

He gave her his bundle to carry, and walked on before

her, according to the Indian custom. At last they reached a hill, from whence they could discern the smoke from the encampment curling up in the air at some little distance amidst the wooded banks of a broad stream. Then the girl sat down at the foot of a tree, and telling her lover that it would not be correct for them to enter the camp together, she begged him to proceed thither alone, while she remained behind for a time.

Thus admonished he walked on alone, and on arriving at the encampment was received by his parents with sad and solemn looks.

"What has happened?" he asked. "Why do you look so sorrowful?"

Neither of them answered him. He turned to his favourite sister, and begged her to go and seek his betrothed, and bring her to the camp.

"Alas!" cried the young girl, "how can I bring her? She has been dead for several days."

The relátions of his intended bride then surrounded him, weeping and groaning, but he would not believe their afflicting news.

"I have just left her," he said, "full of life and health and beauty. Come with me, and I will conduct you to her."

He guided them to the tree beneath which he had left her reclining, but she was no longer there; and the light burden she had carried was lying on the ground. The fatal truth flashed upon the young hunter's mind;

the shock was too great for him, and he fell down dead upon the spot.

This simple story is given as nearly as possible in the same words in which it was related to the narrator one evening close to a watch-fire, in an encampment of Indians on the banks of the very river where the strange event was said to have occurred.

THE TWO GIANTS.

AN EASTERN TALE.

THE sun was beginning to disappear behind the mountains, and with the evening breeze came sweet perfumes,
wafted from the surrounding country into the streets
of Bagdad. A youth, apparently about sixteen years
of age, was leaning against the doorway of a house in
a large square. His finely formed features and his
countenance beaming with intelligence, were lighted
up by the brilliant tints of the setting sun. In looking attentively at him, all who saw him felt convinced
that he was not a being to be contented with exercising
through life the unaspiring position of a clerk in some
office, or an assistant to some tradesman, but that,
through some channel or other, he would rise to dis-
tinction. Yet there was a degree of charming sweetness mingling with the boldness and determination
expressed in his face.

He had been standing as described above, for some
little time, when suddenly the sound of horses' feet,
and the clicking of arms, was heard in an adjoining
street. The young Persian cast his eyes in the direc-

The dun-coloured lion lay crouched on the chest of the giant,
lapping the blood from his lacerated breast.

Page 275.

tion of the sounds, and perceived the grand vizier passing, followed by the principal officials of his palace, and a number of military men. Presently a noise was heard in the street on the other side of the square, which seemed to proceed from a crowd of people, and a man, in the garb of a sage, appeared, followed by all his disciples. The two processions met in the middle of the square, passed each other, and went on in opposite directions.

The youth was intently watching them as they disappeared, when an old man, who had opened the door of the house behind him, softly placed a hand on his shoulder.

"You have been gazing at these two processions, the vizier with his officers, and Noushou with his disciples," said he.

"Yes," replied the young man, "and I was debating with myself which I ought to take as my protector, as both have offered to assist my views in life."

"One chooses the tree according to its fruits," observed the old man.

"I know that, father," replied Barzouzeh; "but the difficulty is to choose the fruit itself. The vizier governs entire nations in the name of the caliph; Noushou has gained all the scientific and intelligent over to his doctrines. The one is master by his power, the other by the force of sympathy; which of the two has the best position?"

The old man did not immediately reply, but remained

for a few minutes with his head bent as if endeavouring to recall something to his memory; at length, turning towards Barzouzeh, he said,—

"Do you know the history of the two giants of Cashmere?"

"No, I do not," said the youth.

The old man motioned to him to sit down, and after a short silence commenced thus:—

"During the primeval age of the earth, there lived, in the depths of the valley of Cashmere, two giants, one of them was called *Azam the Terrible*, the other *Nazel the Blessed*. No man dwelt near them, and everything around belonged to them.

"Now at that early period, this world was not what it has since become. The breath of the Almighty had recently bestowed life on terrestrial things; all was still warm from that breath, and a communication existed between all parts of creation. Man understood the air, the earth, the animals, the plants; and besides being their master, he participated in their life.

"One morning when the sun had risen in all its splendour, Nazel the Blessed appeared on the side of the hill. Noble and beautiful as God had created him, he advanced singing:—

"'It is daylight, and I shall descend into the valley to visit my empire; for I love all that exists around me, from the lofty tree to the almost imperceptible flower which blooms in humility amidst the fissures of the rock; from the monarch of the forest to the buzzing fly.

"'It is I who train the wild vines, when they are almost breaking, and seek a support for them; it is I who conduct the rivulets through the parched grass and the withering groves; and who scatter on the arid rock the seeds of flowers, which shall one day cover it as with a festal robe.

"'It is I who sow the soft moss of which the little birds form their nests; and when the great lion from his mountain den makes the air resound with his roars, it is I who withdraw the thorn which has wounded his mighty paw.

"'All nature knows me, and loves me. I am like the protecting spirit of all things. I am obeyed because I teach to every creature what may be useful to itself, and my superiority does nothing but good.'

"Thus sang Nazel the Blessed, as he appeared amongst the forest glade. Then another voice came, like a storm blast from the summit of the mountain, and it sang:—

"'It is daylight, and I shall descend into the valley to visit my empire; for all that I behold around me is submissive to my will, and I destroy anything that ventures to oppose it, from the slender reed to the mighty tree.

"I force my path through the forest with fire and sword. I split the rocks asunder, and crowd the deepest rivers with their fragments. My arrows can reach the

T

wild birds in the highest eyries, where they gather
their broods beneath their wings.   The great dun-
coloured lion had a companion; I strangled her with
my arms, and her skin hangs as a trophy from my
shoulder.

"'Thus all nature respects and fears me, for I am
like the hurricane that destroys all before it; I am
obeyed because I can annihilate everything; my superiority is a heavy yoke to every created object.'

"Thus sang Azam the Terrible, holding in one hand
his murderous arrows, while his formidable axe swung
at his side.   He wended his way along a narrow gorge
amidst the mountains, through which a rapid stream
was flowing.   But suddenly an immense fig-tree ob-
structed his path.

"It had been planted there by Omnipotence when
the world was first created, and its roots having buried
themselves on both sides of the river, formed an arch
over the water, from the centre of which rose the lofty
trunk.

"Azam scowled at the tree with an angry glance.
'You shall not have stopped me for nothing,' he exclaimed; and seizing his axe, he commenced hacking
at the colossal tree.   At every blow of the axe the poor
tree seemed to groan in secret agony, but Azam struck
on without pity, for he never pardoned the semblance
of opposition.   At length the fig-tree fell, and was
partly split open in its fall.   Azam seized the two
sides of the partially opened trunk to tear them

asunder, but the tree, exerting all its strength, reunited itself, and the hands of the giant remained fast imprisoned. Then a murmur of revolt appeared to arise from all creation. The breeze carried the cries of Azam the Terrible as far as the den where his enemy, the lion, was asleep : the rocks reverberated the cries as if to guide the course of the wild beast. Arrived at the margin of the river he stopped, afraid of its roaring leaping waters ; but the river instantly became tranquil and permitted him to pass. Azam perceived him advancing, and made another powerful effort to free his hands. It was too late; the claws of the king of the desert were already dug into his shoulder. A fearful shriek was heard. A terrible groan, and then all was silent. The dun-coloured lion lay crouched on the chest of the giant, and lapping the blood from his lacerated breast.

" A prolonged murmur of triumph seemed to agitate all the trees, to rush along the slopes of the hills, to swell in the gushing of the water, and to rise into the air, like a sigh of deliverance heaved by universal Nature.

" It was interrupted by the song of Nazel the Blessed, who was returning from the forest. Suddenly there was stillness around ; the breeze played gently before him to refresh his brow ; the river sank into the fairy melody of the faintest ripple. And the trees showered their perfumed blossoms over his head. But Nazel started and stopped short when he reached the entrance of the ravine, for he then perceived the dead body of the other giant. The lion raised his stately head, and Nazel drew back affrighted. But the eyes of the fierce animal softened instantaneously, he wiped off the blood that stained his mouth, and bounding joyously forward, he crouched like a faithful dog at the feet of his former benefactor.

" Then was heard a mysterious voice, which said :—

" ' There is no true power except that which is gained by the superiority of mind: and no durable influence but that which is founded upon love.' "

When the old man had finished his tale, the youth remained for a time plunged in a deep reverie. But on the following day he enrolled himself as one of the disciples of the wise and virtuous Noushou.

In the course of time his name became celebrated throughout Persia for his learning and intelligence, and it was he who compiled a book containing an epitome of human wisdom, which was attributed to one of the leading philosophers of the age.

THE END.